MW00461538

One Western Town
PART 1

The Beginning

DAVID QUELL

LifeRich Publishing books may be ordered through booksellers or by contacting:

LifeRich Publishing
1663 Liberty Drive
Bloomington, IN 47403
www.liferichpublishing.com
844-686-9607

ISBN: 978-1-4897-4605-4 (sc)
ISBN: 978-1-4897-4604-7 (e)

Library of Congress Control Number: 2023900207

Print information available on the last page.

LifeRich Publishing rev. date: 01/17/2023

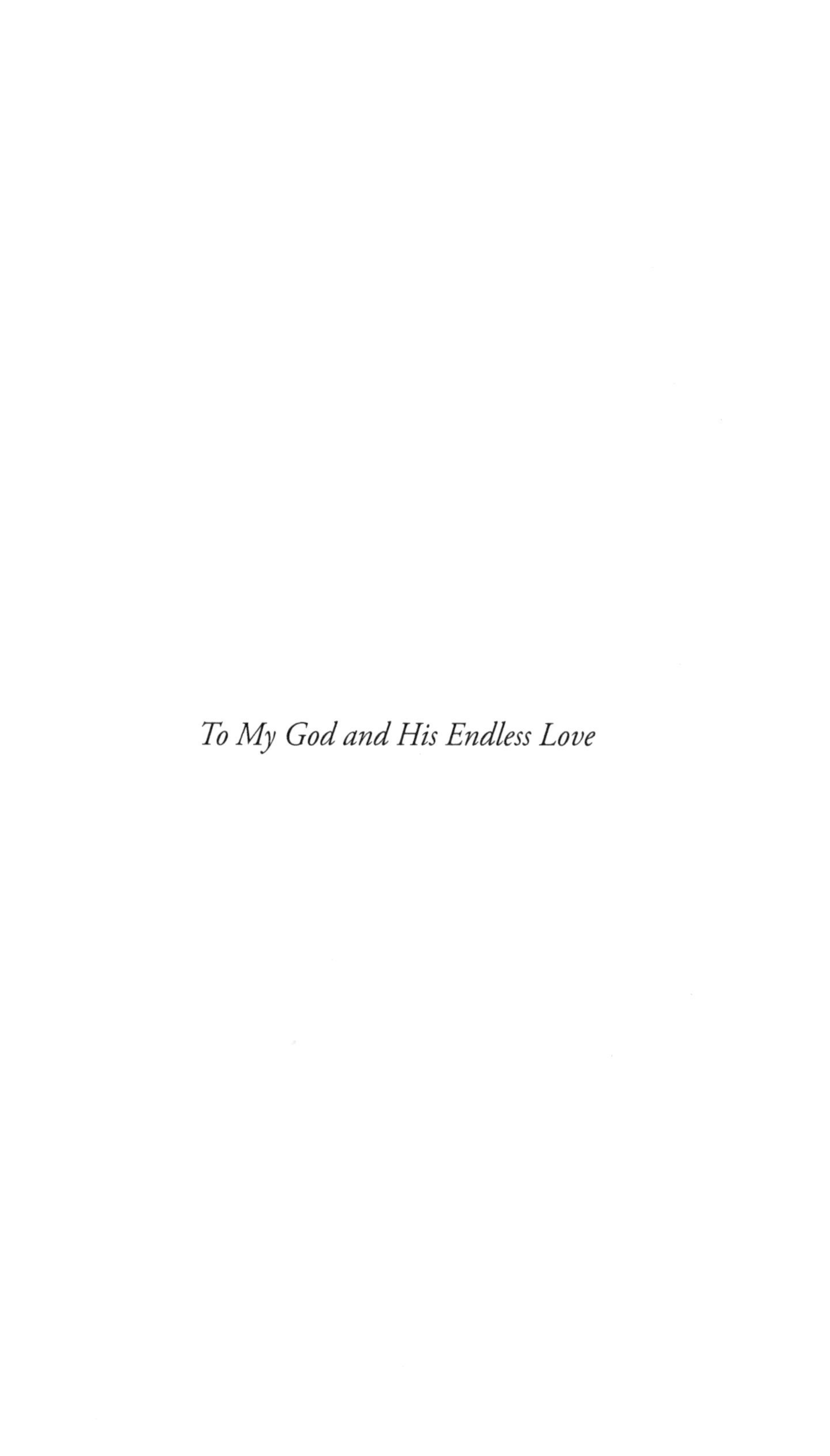

To My God and His Endless Love

Chapter ONE

'I waited patiently for the Lord, and He inclined unto me, and heard my cry. He brought me up also out of a horrible pit, out of the miry clay, and set my feet upon a rock, and established my goings. And He has put a new song in my mouth, even praise unto our God. Many shall see it, and fear, and shall trust in the Lord. Blessed is the man that maketh the Lord his trust, and respecteth not the proud, nor such as turn aside to lies.' (Psm 40:1).

In a past time a boy was born. He was a boy not unlike many others born of Midwestern mothers and fathers. His name was Matthan Quaid. He entered the world loud and large. His truths were constant. His circumstances were not. As a child he knew much charity. He experienced the softness that is shown a child. His naïveté was the jewel of jubilance that occurred but once in a lifetime. The unparalleled exaltation of innocence was the joyance when wonder met discovery. Matthan rejoiced in being loved. He loved his parents and they loved him. No happiness was higher. The splendor was painted on his incessant smile. To Matthan, then, love was the only rule.

As the boy grew, more rules were made. His upbringing was strict, but fair. He was unfailing in his faithfulness to God. Matthan honored his mother and his father. He listened to his mother's and father's words. He lived by God's law. He was a devout son. Each night he knelt and prayed. His favorite was the 23rd psalm. 'The Lord is my shepherd, I shall not want. He maketh me to lie down in green pastures. He leadeth me beside still waters. He restoreth my soul. He leadeth me in the paths of righteousness for his name's sake. Yea, though I walk through the valley of the shadow of death, I will fear no evil; for thou art with me. Thy rod and thy staff, they comfort me. Thou preparest a table before me in the presence of mine enemies. Thou anointest my head with oil, my cup runneth over. Surely goodness and mercy shall follow me all the days of my life, and I will dwell in the house of the Lord forever.' (Pam 23).

Over time the toddler became a schoolboy. Matthan was eager to learn. He yearned for knowledge. He strove to be the best. He was perceptive and inquisitive. He was creative and artistic. To make his parents proud, he worked hard. Matthan entered his academy days and quickly learned to read. He wrote well but was left hand dominant. His penmanship was clear and precise. However his teacher saw the southpaw as being nefarious. The use of the left hand was ungodly. It was regarded as the hand of the devil. Prejudice turned sinistral into sinister. The teacher corrected Matthan with a ruler's rap on the knuckles. Yet Matthan persisted. Each attempt resulted in a more severe beating. With every blow the educator shouted at Matthan to use his right hand. The sharp wood split the skin and cracked the bone. Matthan continued to complete the letters beautifully, as the red drops dripped down onto the paper of white. The caning caused his joints to become swollen and sore. When Matthan recommenced, the stick struck. This happened over and over until the pain forced his fingers to stop.

The bell rang. The assault ended. Matthan made his way home

slowly as the nerve fibers fired up and down his arm. The throbbing pains shallowed his pace. The blood rolled down and stained the cuff of his shirt. The edema distorted his digits. It impeded their motion so that he could not close his fist. He arrived home and entered the house. He immediately heard a cry come from the kitchen.

"Matthan come help me please," his mother shouted.

Matthan worked his way there. He saw a pile of dirty dishes waiting for him. He reached out with his broken left hand, displaying the brutality.

"What happened?" his mother asked.

"I tried to write with my left hand, and my teacher did not like it," Matthan replied.

His mother turned away and pulled off her apron. She thrust it on the table, infuriated. She stormed out of the door like a whirlwind. Mrs. Quaid marched directly to the school. Upon entering the classroom, she briskly strode up to Matthan's instructor. Her wild eyes told the whole story.

"You will not lay your hands, or anything else for that matter, on my boy!" she shouted in anger. " Understand!"

The teacher took a step back as she was sternly stared down. The cold glare sent a shiver through the educator's spine.

"Enough said!" Mrs. Quaid bellowed. Then, without hesitation, the matriarch made her exit.

Times changed. And with change often comes strife. Matthan's simplistic existence became complex. Contradictory actions disrupted his life. His father took to drink. Addiction drove a stake of dependence into his heart. It enslaved his soul, and slowly incinerated it to ash. Desolation and despair dragged down his wretched heart until he drowned in despondency. All hope evaporated. Heartache became heartbreak. Everything was lost but misery. Sadness spiraled into anger. The rage ratcheted up as irascibility ensued, causing harm. The death dealing of alcoholic ingestion ripped and tore. Slash after slash came. Gash after gash came. Matthan bore his father's terrible attacks.

Matthan took refuge in the Word. He prayed.

"'Be merciful unto me, O God. Be merciful unto me for my soul trusteth in thee. Yea, in the shadow of thy wings will I make refuge, until these calamities be overpast.'" (Psm 56:1).

God's eternal love remained omnipresent. The strength of God's devotion created intimacy. God's goodness cut through the violence. Matthan's belief in God drove out the barbarism. The sweet angel of God's affection gave Matthan the desire to endure. With the love of God, he grew strong. He grew strong in spirit.

Matthan lived in his father's world of chaos. His anxiety increased like the empty bottles of booze. His father became removed, then remote. In the end, his father was nonexistent. Each evening the scene seemed to repeat. His father drank. His mother cried. Matthan locked himself away. Isolation is never a boy's best friend. Loneliness loomed inside his room. Solitary confinement weighted mightily on Matthan. Acumen deserted him. His fragile psyche demanded some distance. So, he escaped from the house for hours without permission. The repetition of disobedience led to pride in his impropriety. He lauded his ingenuity, as the conceit made his soul rot. The spoiling spread from inside to out. Insubordination swelled over into mischief and immorality.

Matthan's pals from the street gathered in their clubhouse. Their names were James, William, and Scott. Their gang was called the Burlington Boys. Each boy went by a nickname. They were Jimmy, Billy, Scotty, and Matty. Only club members called the boys by these tags. Their clubhouse was erected in the expanse of an old apple orchard. It had a solid plank floor supported by the trunk of a tree. The walls were somewhat upright. These vertical sides enclosed the edges of the deck. There was no ceiling. Above, there was only leaves, branches, and sky. It was a crude build of wood and nail, nestled in the nectar of a fruit bearing farm. But it was home.

Theodore was a new recruit. He was a little younger than the gang's general age. Theodore admired the Burlington Boys. He longed to be included. But to be a Burlington Boy, one had to pass a test. Matthan told Theodore that he would be welcomed if he could overcome the trial. Theodore agreed to the tryout. Matthan instructed him to come to the clubhouse at noon the next day for the initiation.

It was hot, uncomfortably hot. The heat poured over Theodore like lava. Sweat dripped down the side of his face. His hair was wet. The perspiration covered the path of tears that flowed from his fear. His eyes were red, and his breaths were quick. Theodore felt an immense discomfort. It was worse than wearing his Sunday church clothes. In a great fidget, Theodore waited at the base of the tree. He dreaded this day. The enigma intensified his stress. The not knowing turned his stomach sour. After what seemed like hours, Theodore saw Matthan climb down.

"Are you ready?" Matthan asked.

"Yes, I guess," replied Theodore sheepishly.

Up the ladder they went. Matthan led and Theodore followed. To Theodore, it felt like an execution not an inauguration. Once inside, Matthan told Theodore to take a seat. There was only one chair. Theodore sat. The boys bound him. His anxiety heightened. A cloth was tightened around his head obscuring his vision. Theodore squirmed like a worm on a hook. All of his senses surged. He could smell the fruit. It was a sickly sweet scent. Theodore heard a rhythmic rustling of whispers which resounded like a chant. He felt the sensation of ants crawling across his skin as a numbing cold made him shake. Matthan walked up to where Theodore was tied.

"I have in my hands a grasshopper and a cockroach," said Matthan. He held out his fists, tightly closed. " Now, you will choose the one which you will eat."

Theodore struggled. The boys steadied his chair.

"I cannot! " screamed Theodore.

"Then I will choose for you," said Matthan.

Theodore wrestled to get free, but could not. Matthan forced open his mouth. He placed the contents of his hand onto Theodore's tongue. Theodore spit. In horror, he spit, and spit again. The boys all laughed.

"Let me loose," cried Theodore.

The boys released his hands. Matthan dropped the blindfold, as his smile widened. In his hand he held a small piece of apple.

"It was just a joke," said Matthan.

Theodore stood.

"Not funny," he stammered. " I thought you were my friend!"

"I am," replied Matthan.

"Friends protect each other," said Theodore wiping away his tears.

Theodore rushed down the ladder of the clubhouse.

"It was just a game!" shouted Matthan from above.

Theodore reached the ground and ran. In remorse, Matthan immediately followed. He raced after Theodore engaging his full heart in the effort. Matthan over took Theodore. He grabbed his arm to impede his progress. Theodore stopped. He looked at Matthan with bloodshot eyes.

"Don't worry, I won't tell," cried Theodore.

"Teddy," said Matty. " Forgive me. You are right. I am sorry."

Theodore hesitated.

"You called me Teddy," he replied.

"Yes I know," said Matty. "Because you are my friend."

Matty smiled at Teddy. Teddy smiled back.

"Follow me, I will make this right," said Matty.

Matty walked towards his home. Teddy slowly followed. Matty entered a shed of tools. He located a sledgehammer. He handed the hammer to Teddy. Teddy gave him a blank stare.

"Trust me," said Matty.

He started back to the clubhouse. The strong sun scorched the surface below their feet. The boys felt the heat rise from the incinerated crust. The resultant waves rolled over them. It increased their effort to breathe. It was ever so hot. They arrived at the clubhouse to find it abandoned. Matty fixed his gaze on Teddy. Teddy regarded him.

"Okay my friend," said Matty. " Bring it down!"

Teddy grinned as he started the demolition.

"Teddy, you are more important to me than this… this thing. It is time I show you that."

The boys tore down the construct and flung the pieces to the ground. It was life-changing.

Time moved forward as time does. As it moved, time created a new beginning. Matthan was reborn. A friend's love had pulled him forward. He was content. He smiled. He even laughed. The welcomed news continued when Matthan's father found employment. He stopped drinking. He spent time with his family. It was a warm season. Matthan cherished it all.

When the summer sun softened into fall, a new school year started. Pencils, paper, erasers, protractor, and notebooks were collected for use in his education. The items were gathered in one great pile on Matthan's desk. He sat and stared at the mound. Part of him hoped he could move the monstrosity with just his mind. He did not have the pockets, or the arms for that matter, to carry it all. Hope gave into reality and Matthan plunked himself onto the floor, dejected. A knock at the door interrupted his disappointment. He rose to answer it. Upon opening, his father stood at the entranceway.

"May I come in?" his father asked.

"Yes," replied Matthan.

As the older Quaid entered, Matthan saw that he was carrying a knapsack.

Matthan grinned. " Is it for me?"

"Yes it is for you," replied his father.

"Thank you, thank you Pappy," shouted. Matthan.

"My pleasure, son," he said. "It is new, so I expect you to keep it as such. I worked hard to earn this for you."

"I will. I promise," said Matthan.

The first day of school shone bright with a glorious morning sun. The burning ball ascended with great possibilities. The prospects of a new start were seeded in his mind. Matthan was reinvigorated by the fuel of grateful gratitude. He strutted off to class with confidence and a brand new backpack full of dreams.

Matthan walked through the beams of early light. The day's dew licked up moisture onto his shoes. The softened grass created a padded pathway for his feet. He was alone but not lonely. He imagined an earth filled with flowers. He reached out his hand to touch the petals. The beauty of the blossoms dazzled. The chroma of each stem enhanced the emerald color reflected in his eyes. He glowed. Matthan drew in the succulent scent that surrounded him. The smell was of a sweet perfume. His daydream took him to his past. He remembered his mother seated in her dressing room. Her hair was up, and pulled tight. It was dark and full bodied. She wore a long decorative wrapper. The dress was covered in roses of red and pink. The drape fit loosely, and it hung down daintily to the floor. In her hand she held an atomizer. He saw her squeeze the bulb just slightly to the side of her form. The vapor of coumarin filled the air. The aroma was of sweetgrass and cherry leaves. Matthan felt like he had seen an angel. Standing still he could almost hear the celestial chorus sing. He smiled.

Back on earth, dark cumulus clouds had filled the heavens. Their cauliflower heads swallowed the sun. A group of nasties approached him. The gang blocked Matthan's way. The biggest bully, Julian Johnson, stepped forward. But Matthan felt no fear.

"I have no quarrel with you," said Matthan.

"Not so fast, Quaid," said Johnson. "You see, I am a friend in need. And what I need is a new knapsack."

"You are no friend," replied Matthan.

"Don't be that way Quaid," said Johnson smiling. " I would hate to fight you for it."

"I will not fight," replied Matthan.

"Then hand it over!" Johnson demanded.

Matthan hesitated. He did not want conflict. He wanted to be like the Lord and seek peace. Matthan did not let Julian lure him into a brawl. He pulled the pack from his back and gave it to him. Julian ripped it from Matthan's hand with force.

"Thanks dummy," said Johnson. "Now try not to cry like a little girl," he said laughing.

Matthan held his hatred close. He kept his anger bottled and walked away without lifting a finger.

"The mighty Matthan Quaid, how he has fallen," shouted Johnson as Matthan moved on.

The doleful day blackened as Matthan returned home. He arrived at the front step downtroddened. He turned the handle and pushed open the wooden door. He walked slowly across the living room floor. Out of the corner of his eye he saw his father sitting in his favorite chair. The elder Quaid was reading the newspaper. Smoke from his pipe circled above his head. Matthan wondered why he was home early. He glanced down and saw a glass of liquor on the end table. Next to it was a half empty bottle of whiskey. Hearing the boy's steps, his father lowered the periodical and peered over at him.

"Where's your knapsack?" his father asked firmly.

"I… I lost it," stuttered Matthan, fearful of speaking the truth.

"You lost it!" screamed his father. "What kind of fool loses a pack from his own back?"

He glared at Matthan.

"Come here now!" he shouted.

Unmoved, Matthan responded. "Actually I gave it away."

"What!" exclaimed the elder.

"I gave it to a needy child," continued Matthan in an exaggeration.

"Listen," shouted his father. " I worked hard for that knapsack. Are you telling me that you just gave it away?"

Matthan nodded in the affirmative. His father fumed.

"Go get it back! Go get it back right now or don't come home!"

Matthan hung his head.

"Now get out!" his father yelled.

Matthan made his way back towards school. With each step his fury grew. The anger drove him. Matthan's temperature rose. His eyes began to water as the hatred boiled, flushing his skin. He clenched his fists, escalating his tension. He did not think straight.

The madness muddled his mind. He would tear Julian limb from limb, he thought.

After an hour, the front door of the Quaid family home flung open. A battered and bloodied Matthan walked in. His clothes were tattered and torn. He looked at his father unforgivingly. He thrust the backpack onto the floor.

"There!" exclaimed Matthan.

"Do not address me that way!" shouted his father.

Matthan stared at him in an indignant manner. The green eyes of his Pappy glared back. His son's behavior made him furious. The ferocity turned quickly to violence. Matthan felt the full force of his father's hand as it struck his face. The elder Quaid pulled the belt from his waist and he approached his son.

"You will show respect!" he shouted.

"Do not do this father," Matthan pleaded.

Matthan remained still and took the punishment. All the time he wondered why it had to be so.

In the refuge of his own room, Matthan lay on his bed bleeding. He was too proud to clean himself. He didn't care who saw him in this condition. There was a tap at the door. From it a gentle whisper came.

"My Matty, are you okay?" his mother asked.

"I am fine," replied Matthan. Mrs. Quaid came in and sat on the edge of his bed. She had brought a damp cloth to wipe away the blood. She gazed upon her son with a mournful expression as she worked.

"I am sorry," she said as she washed away the red. After that his mother spoke no more.

Matthan sat in the darkness of his room and soaked in the pain. His wounds were severe, both mental and physical. His father had forced him to fight over a piece of sewn burlap. He was sickened by the thought. The father and son bond was broken. From the fracture, a flood of contempt poured out. Matthan was left isolated. He felt betrayed. How could he honor God's law, he thought. He could not. Matthan put pen to paper. He wrote.

Dear Mother,

The Bible says to honor thy father and thy mother. This I can no longer do. So, I am leaving. Do not look for me.

M.

After the death of dusk, at midnight, Matthan moved slowly. He moved very, very, slowly across the room. He was very, very, dreadfully nervous. The shutters were shut tight. The drapes were drawn. It made for a lack of light. In the black of the pitch his senses were heightened. And into the thick of it he thrust himself. The sound of his shuffling feet puffed up from the planks of the floor. He neither raised or lowered them as he went forward. His was not the festinating gait of a madman. The walk was direct, deliberate. It was a designed gradual migration that he employed. It was not an action of instability but a rational, incremental inching, he exercised.

Matthan heard the beating of his heart. It was strong. The pounding pulse resonated into his head. Each motion he took magnified the rhythm. Booming and drum-like, it repeated. Forcefully it filled his throat, and choked the air from his lungs. Breathe, breathe, breathe, he thought. His psychosis slowed his progress. Yet he moved on.

At last Matthan broke from the confines of his room. He entered the hall with stealth. He headed for the stairs. At the top of the steps he heard a cry. The wailing came through the air with sorrow. Upon hearing the weeping lament, Matthan became as ice. He stood silent, worried his parents would wake and find him there. Matthan was petrified. No one came. He decided to backtrack and calm his baby brother. The nightman hurried down the hall. He entered the nursery in an instant. Matthan found himself standing over a crib containing his sibling. He reached out and gently picked up the child.

"Hush little brother," he whispered. "Shhhhh..."

Matthan cradled him in his arms.

"I am sorry to leave you," he said softly. "But I cannot wait for Pappy to change any longer. Please forgive me my love."

Matthan smiled. As he looked down, it appeared to him that his brother smiled back. A feeling of serenity spread over Matthan. This is true happiness, he thought. Matthan placed his brother back into the bassinet. A sadness ensued as Matthan realized he would not see him again. The loss of love made Matthan's heart heavy. But everything has an end and a beginning.

TWO

Matthan ran. And he kept running. The young Quaid followed the sun. He rose with the day star and traveled west as it crossed the sky. Sol's fire warmed him in a blanket of radiant gentility, like a mother's love. Invigorated by the light, he moved through the countryside without impediment. The land was of rolling hills. It was filled with trees and leaves of green. The breeze was soft and cooling. Matthan filled his lungs with it. With each exhale there came an easing of existence, a feeling of inner peace. He drifted like a feather. Like a never landing plume, he remained afloat.

Matthan lived off the land. Finding fresh water was easy, as streams were plentiful. Fire was created and extinguished. He ate what he caught. Each meal he made sure to give thanks to God. He had only one luxury. He kept it close to his heart. Matthan carried a pocket sized Bible in his coat. While the morning's dew dried, he read. 'They that wait upon the Lord shall renew their strength. They shall mount up with wings as eagles. And they shall walk and not faint.' (Isaiah 40:31). Matthan was a solitary man, but he was never alone. God was with him.

Now and again, Matthan came across a small town. He often traded a day's work for a hot meal. Sometimes it reminded him of home. Matthan did not stay in one spot for long. He kept moving. Guided by God, Matthan went west. He left the burdens of the past behind, like the shedding of skin cells. Venturing into the wilderness took him on a path of revival. Everything he touched, everything he saw was for the first time. The scenery was fresh. The air was ripe. The sky was clear. Birds sang a different song. All was original. Matthan took comfort in the variations.

Coming across a gradient pass, Matthan saw a multitude of tents. White canvas sprang from the soil like pilings of salt. The shaved angles shivered in the sun. It sparkled like a sheet of silver and glass. Matthan marveled at the high-flying flags. Each banner blew distinctively. The colors streamed like a rainbow of cloth signaling the wonderment below. Matthan approached. The site amused him. He grinned as he saw it was the circus.

Matthan entered the compound in a state of amazement. He gazed back-and-forth at the incredible beasts from far-away lands. He saw elephants, tigers, and snakes. There were as many human oddities as there were animals. Clowns, tumblers, trainers, and sideshow attractions abounded all around him. Matthan continued on foot. As he moved, Matthan observed and catalogued. He had heard of such things but to actually see them was a bit of an epiphany.

Matthan came upon a section of a tent that was pulled back. He stuck his head in sideways. Then, he entered. The area under the tapestry was well lit. He could see a gentleman standing near a small table. The man was tall and thin, like a railroad tie. He was well dressed. He wore a waist coat with tails. The coat's color was black, and he had a bright white shirt with a dark cravat. His pants were pressed. A firm crease went down the center. His shoes were leather. He stood straight and had a formal appearance. The man's face was sunken. His high cheekbones protruded out from the dark rings under his eyes. His hair was short and slightly curly. It was parted to one side. The coiled tuffs were a deep brown like his eyes. Matthan came closer. He saw that the table was covered with knives. Some of them seemed familiar. While others were strangely unknown. The sight stunned him for a second. He stood fixed. Then, the gentleman beckoned him over.

"Come in," he said with a Scottish accent.

Matthan held fast.

"Are you in, or are you out?" he asked.

Uncertain, Matthan made his way towards the table cautiously. His eyes bounced from side to side looking for a possible exit.

"Do not be afraid," he said. "I am merely a showman."

The gentleman lifted his arm and directed an open hand to the table.

"This is my craft."

Swallowing his fear, Matthan walked right up to him.

"I am Andrew," said the gentleman. "I am master of the sharp arts here at the circus."

Matthan did not understand. His expression gave the impression of a lack of comprehension. Andrew continued.

"I am billed as the Warrior Brit. My lovely assistant over there is Ella. She is my target girl."

Matthan glanced to his right. Standing next to a large rounded bullseye was a young girl of great beauty. She had long black hair. It was stationary and straight like the night's air. Matthan looked deep into her amber eyes. Her smile left him spellbound, but uneasy in a way. A cold tremor traveled down to his toes. His cheeks became flushed. Frozen in fire, Matthan turned away, wary that she would read his emotion.

Andrew stepped in to relieve the tension.

"Thank you, Ella," he said. "That will be all for today."

The slender gentleman pulled out a chair.

"Shall we sit?" he asked.

Matthan sat and Andrew followed suit. To quell his fidget, Matthan interlocked his fingers. He squeezed tightly and tried not to squirm. Andrew placed his gloved hands flat on the table. Matthan peered over at him out of the corner of his eye. Andrew held his right wrist still. The digits were unmoving.

"I see you have noticed my deformity," he said.

Matthan slumped in his chair.

"It is okay laddie. You do not offend me."

Andrew pulled off his right hand and placed the prosthetic down on the table with a thud.

"It is wood," said Andrew.

"What happened?" asked Matthan.

"I lost it in a fencing match," replied Andrew. " Laddie let me tell you the story. I was a champion. A challenge came from a man by the name of Daghishat Engel. He was not an honorable man. I can still see it all so clearly. The early day's light illuminated the haze. The fog seemed like a clouded dream. The vapor enveloped London in a veil of wet mist. The atmosphere left a thin film on my skin. I strode through the streets lost in my miasmal mind. I could not concentrate. I was mired in introspection. Even as a master I felt unfulfilled. In my fractionated state, I walked to Southwark on the southern bank of the Thames. Most matches took place at a Salle. This day, however, we were to meet at the old Beargarden."

"Beargarden?" inquired Matthan.

"It was an amphitheater constructed hundreds of years ago. It was a circular stone structure open at the top. It had tiers of benches that surrounded a fighting pit. Bears were chained to the floor and attacked by armed men. It was savage. There was no honor in it."

"So why go there?" asked Matthan.

"Dag wanted an arena that accommodated the greatest number of people." replied Andrew.

"And you agreed?" asked Matthan.

"Yes," replied Andrew. " I felt a champion should accept all challenges. And he was a good swordsman... But his skill was markedly surpassed by his enormous ego."

Matthan smiled broadly as he held back his laughter.

"It was a duel with sabres," said Andrew.

"Sabres?" asked Matthan.

"It is a blade with cutting edges on both sides. The saber has a pointed tip for thrusting. The hilt has a smooth bell that wraps below the grip to the pommel. Its design was to prevent injury to the hand without hindering performance. It is a lovely weapon but its design did not prevent what happened."

Andrew paused as the words took him back in time. He picked up the sabre from the table. He stared up and down the sword.

"You see, there was no director at the Beargarden. With no director, there was no concern for one's behavior. There was no ruling on lines or footing. There was no one to interpret or question the calls. It was a duel of honor. But he had none."

Andrew placed the sword down, then he continued.

"I saluted and took the en garde position. Dag aimed his sabre at me with his arm fully extended. He called out 'Allez!' Like a bang came his advance. Lunge after lunge came his attack. The blades engaged as I parried."

"Parried?" asked Matthan.

"Yes, you know, countered," replied Andrew.

Matthan was lost in the language. Andrew hesitated in an effort to allow the information to travel and process. It did not.

"Okay, laddie," said Andrew. " I will draw down on the floridity."

"Floridity?" questioned Matthan.

"Yes laddie," replied Andrew. "The flowery language."

"Please do," said Matthan. " It is like listening to a snake hiss."

"I will endeavor to do better," said Andrew. "Dag did not fight fair. He fashioned a false attack in an effort to deceive me. Frustrated by his lack of results, Dag followed with an aggressive fletche. It is an illegal lunge in sabre dueling. I blocked using septime. He passed by me with a strong corps a corps. You would call it a body blow. My hand was still supinated and exposed. Dag drew his saber across my wrist with force. He severed all it's bands. Blood poured forth like a red river. I lost all feeling, motion, and strength. I dropped my sword and clutched my dying hand. 'Submit,' he said. 'You dodger! You should forfeit!' I cried. Dag took his sabre and touched it to my forehead. 'Touche,' he said. 'Score one. It's over.'"

Andrew looked down where his hand used to be. He peered directly into Matthan's eyes.

"All the connections had been cut. The surgeon could not save my hand. The remaining threads were clipped. All I have now is this stump," said Andrew sadly.

"I am sorry, sir," said Matthan.

"I walk in faith my friend. I overcame my sorrow long ago," said Andrew. "And please, no need to call me sir. Just call me Andrew.

"Can you teach me to fence?" asked Matthan excitedly.

"After all that?" he questioned.

"Yes," replied Matthan firmly.

Andrew gazed fondly at the boy.

"Okay then," said Andrew. "I will teach you all I know about swords and knives."

Matthan's face lit up like a sparkler.

"It's getting near showtime," said Andrew. "Come back tomorrow morning and we will begin then."

"I cannot," said Matthan. " I have no home," he said sadly.

"Then you shall stay with me," said Andrew.

Matthan nodded his head. Andrew walked towards the exit.

"Come, you can stay in my tent. It is modest, but you can find comfort there."

The two stepped into the natural light. The circus grounds were busy. Entertainers and animals of all forms and curiosities flowed around them. Andrew made his way through the stream of performers. Matthan followed. The pair came across a mountain of a man made of pure muscle. He was seven feet tall. He was shirtless and bald. The brute wore black tights to the waist, and matching boots. The giant held his hand up to stop Andrew.

"So, who do we have here?" asked the strongman.

"This is Matthan, my apprentice," replied Andrew.

The strongman put out his hand to shake with Matthan.

"Good to know you," he said. "My name is Goliath."

"Like in the Bible?" asked Matthan.

"Yes," said Goliath. "Like in the Bible."

The strong man smiled, accentuating his handlebar mustache. Matthan grinned and shook his hand.

"My name is Matthan," said the boy. "Good to greet you, sir."

Goliath let out a whale of a laugh.

"I've been called many things, but never sir," he said.

The colossus turned towards Andrew.

"I like this apprentice of yours," he said.

Andrew acknowledged the giant. Then he continued through the tumult. They passed animals, artists, acrobats, musicians, fascinations, and mimes. Matthan and Andrew came to a small canvas shelter. Andrew opened the entrance for Matthan.

"Here we are," he said.

"Thank you," responded Matthan.

The quarters were spartan. Matthan looked to and fro. He saw pillows, blankets, and a tiny chair. The chair had a matching wooden desk. Its legs were made of metal. They were so thin that Matthan imagined that a small puff of wind could toss it. In the corner he saw a cot.

"It is humble, but it is home," said Andrew.

Matthan faced his benefactor.

"I am grateful," said Matthan sincerely.

"The cot is yours," said Andrew. " I will obtain another, then I will return."

Matthan set his heavy pack down. It dropped like stones. He lay on the cot, supine. He closed his eyes. He slept. In his slumber, the day turned to night. Darkness filled the tent. Bright beams of moonlight crawled under the corners of the cloth. The shimmer created a liquid look on the floor. The limpid appearance gave him a sense of buoyancy. The canvas seemed separated from the ground. He hovered. Matthan was weightless. In flight, he left his body. The boy broke earth's bonds, and climbed slowly into the clouds. It was glorious. He floated. A gentle breeze blew him higher. He soared. Matthan looked across the tops of trees, and down through the plains. His aura drew him toward the ambient fluid of the moon. His ethos mixed with the essence of the atmosphere. Matthan's spirit seemed to illuminate the hills and valleys in silver. He glided over the reflection of the shiny scenery with a sense of serenity.

The new sun carried in the day. The dawn brought another beginning for Matthan. He opened his eyes to see Andrew sitting quietly, sipping a hot cup of coffee. A scalding steam rose off the top.

"Good morning," said Andrew.

"I hope so," replied Matthan.

The Warrior Brit smiled at Matthan in affirmation.

"With God in it, every day is beautiful," Andrew said steadfastly.

Matthan sat up.

"I agree," Matthan replied. "'He hath made everything beautiful in his time.'" (Ecclesiastes 3:11).

"Can I offer you a cup of coffee?" asked Andrew.

"No, thank you. Water would be great though," responded Matthan.

Andrew placed his cup down and ducked outside for a minute. He returned with a identical tin cup full of clear liquid.

"Water, as you requested," said Andrew.

He handed the mug to Matthan. He drank.

"Are you hungry?" asked Andrew.

"Very much so," said Matthan.

Andrew turned to the small table inside the tent. There were several clumps of bread wrapped in a cloth atop the stand. He opened it and gave a piece to Matthan. The lad bowed his head in a silent prayer. Afterwards, he ate without interruption or conversation.

Matthan wiped the crumbs from his face. Then he brushed the excess from his clothes.

"What shall we do next?" asked Matthan.

"I teach, and you learn," replied Andrew.

"Yes!" the anxious youth exclaimed.

Andrew took Matthan to the training tent. It was packed full of circus folk. They were tall, small, and in between. Matthan recognized Goliath as he raised a bar of heavy weights over his head. The strongman had worked hard. The excessive sweat glistened on his skin as he flexed and strained. The behemoth grinned when he glimpsed Matthan. The lad waved with enthusiasm. Matthan looked around the arena. As he gazed up, he saw men and women swinging from a bar. The acrobats glided with ease. Underneath the trapeze were painted horses. They whirled about in circles. Their riders were decorated in flamboyant costumes. The horsemen and women twirled, stood, spun, and leapt from side to side. It was mesmerizing.

Andrew led Matthan to his table. The surface was covered with throwing knives. Each was a different size, shape, and weight. A short distance away was a wooden target. A red dot was is in the center. The bullseye had multiple indentations from previous strikes.

Andrew lifted his sleeve to his mouth. He bit the cuff and pulled it back. Matthan seemed surprised. He had forgotten that Andrew had only one hand.

"Now we embark on your education," said Andrew. "Start with the longer knives. They are easier to throw."

Andrew threw. Then Matthan threw. They threw, and threw. They threw, and threw. And then they threw some more. Matthan struggled to get it right. Andrew directed him with patience. Matthan increased his effort. Andrew encouraged him.

"Good!" shouted Andrew when Matthan hit the mark. "You are showing remarkable improvement. But let us stop for today. We must rest."

And with that, Andrew led his apprentice away in silence.

Days became weeks. Weeks became months. Andrew carried in an elongated chest to the practice tent. He lifted the lid revealing three swords. Andrew grabbed the foil with his one hand.

"What is that?" asked Matthan.

"A foil," replied Andrew.

"Really? It looks more like a needle with a handle," said Matthan with a chuckle.

"It is made for fencing," said Andrew.

"That tiny pin?" laughed Matthan.

"Let me demonstrate," said Andrew.

The master swung around placing his feet at right angles. They were approximately three feet apart and his knees were bent. Andrew had his left foot forward. He raised the foil to a forty-five degree angle. Andrew lunged. In a few quick movements he serrated Matthan's shirt. The lad's top became a perforated rag. Andrew stepped back and withdrew.

"Again, we start," said Andrew. "Which is your strong hand?" Andrew asked.

"My left," said Matthan.

"Great! As you can see, I have but a left hand, so it is a good place to begin," Andrew laughed.

The two trained every day. Before each session Andrew would say, "'He which soweth bountifully shall reap also bountifully.'" (2 Corinthians 9:6). Matthan pushed himself to the extreme. Often, he failed. But he would come back with increased intensity. Never did he give in. Andrew challenged him in trial after trial. After months, Matthan decided to give an opening statement of his own.

"I get that you are a disciple of the New Testament. I am more of an Old Testament man," said Matthan with a sly smile. "'He that observeth the wind shall not sow. And he that regardeth the clouds shall not reap.'" (Ecclesiastes 11:4).

"So, you wait for nothing?" asked Andrew sarcastically. "Next you will tell me that you are all fire and brimstone."

"Maybe I am," said Matthan. "Maybe it makes me a hard man."

"Well good," said Andrew. "'Iron sharpeth iron, so a man sharpeth the countenance of his friend.' (Proverbs 27:17). How is that for hardness?"

"Satisfactory," said Matthan with a grin.

After training for months, Andrew asked his apprentice to meet him in the great tent. Matthan went and waited. Under the big top even a large man felt small. Finally, Matthan saw his mentor appear. He carried a box with both arms. Andrew struggled slightly as his one hand tried to balance it. He set the carton down next to Matthan. As Andrew opened the lid, Matthan looked inside. It contained books. It contained several books. It had novels, volumes of philosophy, collections of poems, and manuals of instruction. It had Plato, Byron, Keats, Descartes, Voltaire, and more.

"Here," said Andrew pulling out one of the covered reads. "This is called the Book of Five Rings. Study it. Learn it. Commit it to memory. It will serve as a great adjunct to my teaching."

"Thank you," said Matthan.

"You are most welcome," said Andrew. "And you may take and read any or all of the others as well. Tomorrow we will talk. For it is time to go further than just physical discipline. Laddie, you must accumulate knowledge. That is what leads to true mastery. Today I am the master and you are the apprentice. Tomorrow you will have no master."

Matthan read. Matthan studied. Matthan absorbed the words. He became a master. The day came which found Andrew meeting Matthan at the same spot. The young man replaced a book of sonnets by Shakespeare back into Andrews' collection.

"It is time for you to leave us," said Andrew.

"I know," replied Matthan.

"I love you like my own," said Andrew.

"And I you," said Matthan.

Matthan looked longingly at his mentor. He hugged his hero.

"Please," said Andrew. "Take a book with you. When you turn the pages think of me."

Matthan reached in the box and pulled out Tamberlane and Other Poems, by Edgar Allan Poe.

"I can see that in you," said Andrew. "Be careful though. Do not fulfill your future just yet. Let God guide you in all things."

"'I thank my God upon every remembrance of you,'" said Matthan. (Philippians 1:3).

Andrew chuckled. "There is some New Testament blood in those veins after all."

Chapter THREE

Quaid went west. He followed the setting sun. As he moved the sky seemed more blue. The white clouds accentuated the colors. Fluffy and full, the vaporous tuffs did not obscure the light. Each day seemed more bright. He was happy. His contentment brought forth abundance in his life. He smiled at the small mishaps, and he laughed at the large ones. He walked through the woods with a knife strapped to his hip. On the opposite side he carried a six shooter. Quaid knew nature well. He reveled in its peace but prepared for a fight.

Quaid stopped to camp for the night. He had traveled over hills, across streams, and down paths. He took time to reflect on the day. He took time to give thanks and pray. Quaid rested his head on his knapsack close to the heat of the fire. The flashes danced with hues of orange and blue. In repose the light turned into illusion. Combustive figures came alive. Quaid pictured his friends performing in the flickering glow. The rhythmic motion was mesmerizing. It melted his heart. Quaid felt warm inside his memory. In serenity, he slept.

Quaid hunted. He had to trap game to eat. He had to kill to live. Quaid moved quietly through the brush with his bow and arrow drawn. He came upon a small babbling brook. He understood that prey would come here to drink. He positioned himself above the stream on a flat rock, free from sight. Here, he waited. Hours passed. The sun poured down burning bursts of photons. The energetic particles collided with his skin. The surrounding air grew heavy, as the moisture residing in it thickened. It was like making butter in a churn. Quaid perspired. He wiped his brow, for the droplets did not evaporate. In a pool of sweat, he sat.

The strong force of the day's heat brought another hunter to the water's edge. It was a Native American warrior about Quaid's age. He wore buffalo skin shoes and pants. Shirtless, he was muscular and lean. His hair was dark and pulled back into a tail. He held his bow in one hand as he knelt to drink. The white rapids flowed violently, concealing the surrounding sounds. Quaid remained calm. He heard a low-pitched growl away from the stream. From behind the warrior a grizzly charged. It was big and angry. With his ears near the current, the warrior did not hear the animal approach. Suddenly, it was on him. A great thrashing turned the watercourse red. The brown bear tore the warrior's flesh. Fangs bit into his head and neck. He was going to die. Quaid drew his knife. He leapt from his vantage point right onto the bear's back. In a single motion, Quaid ripped the muscles from the throat to the nape. Hemorrhage sprung like a fountain. The beast reared, reaching for Quaid. It clawed with a savage burst of madness. Quaid dropped behind the creature as it stood. On its hind legs, the bear was massive. It flailed out of control. Quaid ducked down. He reached his blade through to the groin. With all his might, he cut across the big blood vessels pumping there. More red flooded the stream. The bear dropped to its knees. Then it fell over, dead.

Quaid raced to the lifeless warrior. He pulled him from the

water. He put pressure on the wounds. His hands held back the flow. Stained and covered in blood, Quaid tore pieces of his clothing to bind each puncture. He placed his ear to the warrior's chest. His heart was beating. His lungs moved air. He was alive. His injuries were severe. The warrior needed help, and he needed it fast. Quaid's eyes tracked the warrior's path. He lifted the unconscious man atop his shoulders, and moved in double time. With an impassioned quickstep, he dashed past bent branches. He bounded over the ungraded ground. He scrambled up each incline. He was desperate. At the top of a hill, he saw smoke billowing up into the sky. It came from the valley of a nearby plain. Quaid directed his course toward the rising vapor. He was propelled forward with the strength of ten men. His heart pounded as he drew energy from emotion. Quaid's will was unyielding. He pushed harder. Every muscle ached to the point of spasm. Every joint throbbed under the strain. Every step stung, sending a needle prick sensation up from his feet. His arms pained under the weight of a dying man. He pushed on.

Quaid came to a clearing. He saw tipi ahead. He pushed the persuasion of agony out of his head. He forged forward. With hope in his heart, Quaid entered the camp. He was immediately surrounded by warriors. He stopped. Looking around he perceived the danger. The circle of warriors closed. Quaid laid the injured warrior down and stepped away. Upon seeing his traumatic state, Quaid was seized. He made no further movements. An elder broke through the line of men and approached the wounded youngster. He knelt by his side. He spoke a few words but they were unidentifiable. As the elder rose, several warriors rushed in and carried the wounded youth away. The elder approached Quaid. He spoke as he walked. Quaid did not understand his language but he recognized the mask of hatred. Quaid saw the anger behind the elder's eyes. Quaid was forcibly removed. Yards from the encampment was a rounded cage made of wood. The dome-shaped structure appeared like an unfinished wigwam. The circular construct was made of bent saplings. The height was about seven feet and its diameter was twelve. Bark fibers were used to fasten the saplings in a crossed pattern about a foot apart. The strands of vines fixed the connections like cement. The bonded bars were driven deep into the dirt. There was no thatch covering, however. It gave a clear view into the interior. The overturned semicircle was a timbered prison. Quaid had his hands and feet bound. He was cast into the snare. There, he sat in fatigue and frustration, grounded in the cell.

The day stole away into night. Quaid remained captive. An immense bonfire lit up the darkness not far from his detention. The flames grew like a weed into the fertile soil of the sky. Dancing shadows cavorted in a celebration. They fluttered on the background of black. The flickering motion seemed to cast a spell on its audience. Quaid just stared, lost in thought. He watched as a large circle of tribesman formed around the fire. A leader wearing a war bonnet appeared. The headdress was mostly red. The colored feathers transitioned to yellow, white, and black. Drums sounded. They were rhythmic and harsh. The pounding intensified over time. Louder and louder the beat boomed. The vibrations seemed to run in a pattern. They followed along with the path of the warriors. A muscular man stepped forward. From Quaid's view, it appeared as he came straight out of the flames. He was almost six feet tall. His mouth and jaw were covered in white up to his nose. Over that was an imprint of a hand in black. Two dark rectangles paralleled the white area from his eyes to his ears. On the warrior's forehead was a solitary yellow line. It was crooked. It went up, then down. It ended in one last rise and fall, like a lightning bolt. His hair was black, braided, and long. An eagle feather adorned the cords. Long leggings of buckskin covered his legs. Between them was a flap of beachcloth. All was held by a leather belt. Tanned straps wrapped around each leg above the knee. He had no shirt but a breastplate of bones fell from his neck.

Quaid was pulled from his prison by two tribesmen. He was led to the center of the circle. He was to fight. He was bigger and stronger than his opponent. But being bound, he was at a disadvantage. Quaid glared at the warrior. The native fixed his stare upon him. The warrior removed his breastplate and handed it to another. A second came forward and gave him a coup stick. It was a long wooden branch free of bark. It had a curved end with several notches along its length. There was an eagle feather attached at one end. A third came from behind Quaid and cut the shirt from his back. He tossed it into the fire. A lead cross hung around Quaid's neck. It glimmered in the glow of the blaze. The warrior grasped the cross and cut it from Quaid's throat. He threw it into the fire as well. Quaid attempted to retrieve the relic, but he was restrained. He became angered. His muscles tensed. His breathing deepened. His pulse quickened. His anger boiled over to outrage.

The drums stopped. Quaid's adversary moved with a crafty cautiousness. Quaid followed him with his eyes. In a quick burst, the warrior struck him with the stick. A giant roar erupted from the crowd. Quaid looked down and saw a red mark across his ribs. The warrior circled and struck again. This time he smacked Quaid's leg. It stung. He had seen enough. He looked for an opportunity to strike back. The warrior came around and attacked from the front. The coup stick came at his head. Quaid blocked the blow and held the cane firmly in his hands. Using leverage, he spun and turned the warrior away from him. He wrapped the rope from his wrists around the warrior's neck. Quaid dropped back and pulled the warrior down. He applied pressure to his windpipe. Slowly, his opponent succumbed to the lack of oxygen. The warrior fell faint. Quaid threw him away like a bag of garbage. He stood and moved quickly in the direction of the fire. The surrounding tribesmen ran at him. Quaid found his cross sitting on the edge of the embers. He reached with his left hand to pick it up. The molten lead singed his palm. It branded him. Quaid let go of the hot metal. He looked down at the mark. His hand radiated red and became swollen. He saw an upside down crucifix staring back at him. However, if he held it out an onlooker saw the reverse, the cross right side up.

Quaid was crammed back in his cage. He did not understand

their aggressive actions. He only wanted to help. He was exhausted. He sat dejected and in pain. Hours passed. Quaid lay on his side, cold and sore. From behind his head he heard a whisper. It was like the coo of a child. He sat up and looked behind. A young boy attempted to gain Quaid's attention. He slid closer to the boy. Quaid saw that it was not a native, but he was wearing the attire of the tribe.

"I speak English," said the boy.

"Who are you?" asked Quaid.

"They call me Eddie Lost Boy," he said.

"Eddie?" questioned Quaid.

"Yes," he replied. "Because I was found lost in the woods several years ago. Eddie was my given name. I did not speak their language. So, I kept repeating my name, Eddie. The elders combined it to their description to form my name."

"Good to meet you Eddie," said Quaid. "My name is Matthan."

Eddie grinned.

"Can you get me out of here?" asked Quaid.

"Sorry, no," said Eddie. "They would suspect me. I could be killed."

"What then?" asked Quaid.

"Information," Eddie replied. " I can give you information."

"Okay, shoot," said Quaid.

"Old Chief Smoke is angry. He thinks you did this to Red Cloud," said Eddie.

"Red Cloud?" inquired Quaid.

"Yes, the warrior you carried into camp," replied Eddie. "He is still unable to talk."

"I did not injure him," said Quaid sternly. "It was a bear. I was trying to help."

"But they think you are responsible," said Eddie.

"Great," said Quaid sarcastically.

"Tonight was just a test," said Eddie.

"A test?" asked Quaid.

"Yes, a test of a warrior's bravery. That is why he used the coup stick," said Eddie. "But now they have seen you fight. So the contest tomorrow will be to the death."

"Wonderful," responded Quaid with more sarcasm.

"I can translate your words to them. Maybe they will listen," said Eddie.

"And if not?" asked Quaid.

"Then we are both lost," said Eddie.

Night gave way to day. Quaid's mind raced. He slept little. All was quiet around the camp. The flames of the fire had died. The smoldering logs drew their last breaths. The red and orange had turned to gray and black. Quaid had no hunger but his thirst was great. Quaid saw Eddie slowly sneaking towards the cage. He was carrying a cup made of clay. Quaid motioned for Eddie to come closer. Like an angel from heaven, he had brought water. Eddie passed the cup through the tied branches of Quaid's confinement. He gave thanks, and drank it in a gulp. Some of the fluid splashed onto his face as he swallowed. He was renewed.

"I spoke to Old Chief Smoke," whispered Eddie.

"And?" asked Quaid.

"He does not believe you," replied Eddie.

"How is Red Cloud doing?" asked Quaid.

"Unchanged," said Eddie.

"You are full of good news this morning," said Quaid in a tart retort.

"I will do what I can," said Eddie.

"Sorry my friend, I do thank you," said Quaid. " I appreciate your effort."

"Speaking of," said Eddie. "You are to fight again today."

"When?" asked Quaid.

"Midday. When the sun is directly above," replied Eddie.

"Until then I will be in prayer," said Quaid. " I will pray for you as well my friend."

"Thanks. And good luck," said Eddie. The boy smiled at Quaid. "Try to stay alive," he said.

"I plan to," said Quaid. "Now go before someone sees you."

Eddie scampered away. He did not want to go, but he knew that if he stayed the situation could become complicated for both men.

The time fell like grains of sand in an hourglass. Each bit hit with an ever increasing weight. Quaid was burdened more by every moment. He knelt to ease his worry. He prayed.

"' Notwithstanding the Lord stood with me, and strengthened me; that by me the preaching might be fully known, and that all might hear. I was delivered out of the mouth of the lion. And the Lord shall deliver me from every evil work, and will preserve me unto his heavenly kingdom to whom be glory forever and ever. Amen,'" said Quaid. (2 Timothy 4:17-18).

With the sound of the drums, the tribesmen gathered again. The chief sat at the head of the circle. Two warriors were at his side. The stockade was opened. Quaid stepped out from the crate. Warriors led him to the ring. One drew a knife and cut the binds around his hands. The warriors flanking the chief advanced.

"Two against one," whispered Quaid. "Hardly seems fair,"

His opponents were each given a long blade. Quaid glanced around but there was no weapon for him. He looked down at the inverted cross burned into his left hand.

"Lord help me," he whispered.

The drums stopped. The warriors approached. Quaid kept an eye open for any bold movements. From his right, a warrior lunged. He swung his knife. He missed but not by much. With a sidestep, Quaid was able to grab his arm at the wrist. He turned the hand down, shifted his weight, and flung the fighter to the ground. The other struck as the assailant hit the dirt. The prick pained as it drew blood. Quaid delivered a blow to his face. It knocked him down. Quaid ran to his cage. He broke off a piece of the wooden lattice. He held out it in defiance. A warrior charged. Quaid crushed his forearm with the baton, breaking the bones. The warrior dropped his dagger in agony. He followed up with a strike to the head. The wallop rendered the warrior unconscious. The second arose and came at Quaid. He brandished his blade, turning it back and forth. The warrior swung high and hard. Quaid backed away and struck a solid blow to his leg. A crippling sensation exploded up his appendage. The warrior dropped to one knee. Quaid smacked him with force. He fell, incapacitated.

The onlookers shouted loudly. A garrison of warriors moved in to subdue Quaid. The chief came forward and looked at him with disdain. He saw the blood dripping from Quaid's hand. He saw it spill from its source, the charred cross. The old warrior became infuriated. He signaled his tribesmen. The warriors began beating their captive. They dragged Quaid back to his cage and hurled him into it with malice. He hit the ground hard. Quaid hurt. He passed out from the punishment.

Quaid awoke with a whisper. It was Eddie.

"Are you okay?" he asked.

"I am still here," he replied.

"Tell me," said Eddie. "What is that symbol on your hand mean?"

"It is the sign of my Savior," replied Quaid. "He died so that I could live."

"I do not understand," said Eddie.

"God became a man, and He came to earth," said Quaid. "He made blind men see. He made the lame to walk. He healed the sick. And to those who mourned, He comforted. To the poor, He gave bread. And He taught all men the way of God."

"So why did He die?" asked Eddie.

"For sin," said Quaid.

"Sin?" asked Eddie.

"An act of evil against God's law," said Quaid. "The Lord died for all men's disobedience, even my disobedience. He died so that I could be free from my wrongs, and live with God in heaven forever. 'For Christ also hath suffered for sins, the just for the unjust, that he might bring us to God.'" (1 Peter 3:18).

"That is noble," said Eddie.

"Yes," said Quaid. "To die for another is an act of love that cannot be repaid, only accepted."

"And God did this for you?" asked Eddie.

"Yes," said Quaid. "And He did it for you too."

"It is hard to find such love in this world," said Eddie.

"His love is what makes me strong," said Quaid.

"I will speak again to Old Chief Smoke. I will tell him of your God. Maybe he will listen," said Eddie.

"And Red Cloud?" asked Quaid. "Any change?"

"Not yet," replied Eddie.

The boy turned and made his way back to the encampment. Quaid watched his friend drift away from view. Quaid fell back against the wall of the cage. Fatigue overcame him.

The pounding of the drums awoke Quaid like a thunder blast. He had a very uneasy feeling. Twice before the drums boomed. Twice before combat came. Quaid readied himself. The most elder appeared with an ever sullen face. He sat. The sounds ceased. Quaid was again extricated from his cell. They cut the rope that bound his feet. Three warriors stood and awaited him armed with knives and clubs. In a single beat of the drum, they closed in on Quaid. Just as the fighting was about to start, a loud voice shouted out. It was Red Cloud. A pathway through the people opened from him to the chief. Still unsteady, the young warrior stumbled to reached the ruler. Red Cloud instructed the elder and the warriors to cease their aggression. Eddie ran to Quaid. He wrapped his arms around his waist and held tight. Old Chief Smoke and Red Cloud approached Quaid together. The old warrior spoke. Eddie looked up at Quaid.

"He regrets you having to endure this trial," said Eddie.

Quaid let out a sigh of relief.

"Tell him that I am grateful that Red Cloud is well," said Quaid. "And that only the strongest leaders are able to change their minds."

Eddie relayed the message. The chief replied and Eddie translated.

"He said that whatever you can see, it is yours," said Eddie.

"Tell the chief that God teaches me to forgive," said Quaid. "There is no shame in protecting one's family. There is no need for amends."

Eddie relayed the words. Again, the chief responded.

"He said that he was told of your God. He must be great indeed to give you such learning," Eddie conveyed. "And he said you may go with a blessing of good favor and thanks."

Quaid smiled at the leader. He nodded in affirmation of the ruler's words. He then looked at Eddie.

"Ask him if I may stay," said Quaid. " I would like to see Red Cloud make a full recovery. And I would like to learn about his people and their ways."

Eddie paused. He then excitedly passed on Quaid's inquiry. Old Chief Smoke nodded, yes.

Chapter FOUR

The sun dried the morning's dew. Each particle of vapor rose to the heavens in a measured temporal movement. An epochal era of understanding began with one man, Matthan Quaid. He learned the native language with Eddie's assistance. Red Cloud introduced him to their culture. He gave Quaid instruction in the art of hunting and tracking. Being a superb horseman, he taught Quaid his equestrian expertise. Quaid lived it. He participated in the traditions and experienced the community. At every opportunity Quaid spoke of God. He told the stories of love and triumph from the Bible. He often read aloud his favorite passages to Red Cloud. Quaid was better than a friend, he was family. Quaid kept his family like he did the good book, close to his heart. Life was easy. But tribulation did come. Many times found Quaid and Red Cloud defending their land and people. They fought tough battles and they won great victories. As they aged, they were bound in brotherhood, and in God's greater love.

Old Chief Smoke passed on. The young prince, Red Cloud, became the leader of a nation. Quaid supported his brother. He understood Providence. He let God guide him each day. Devine Will had brought him here. He saw it. He knew it. He had prayed for it. God's great design had given him purpose, of that he had no doubt. He spread the Word of God so others could grow. They grew in love.

Seasons changed. The sun and the moon traded places again and again. Peace and prosperity pervaded. Wars and rumors of wars had faded from thought. On an ordinary afternoon, a small contingent of five Westerners arrived in camp. They requested a meeting with Red Cloud. The Westerners had heard of the leader's heroic deeds. Stories had spread from land to land and over open spaces of his virtue and his victories. Words had been spoken and passed on of the Red Prince and his Green-eyed Knight. The Westerners sought an audience. They hoped that Red Cloud would grant their request and offer his help. The Westerners waited patiently for him. A crowd gathered as word of their visit spread through camp. Quaid kept his distance. He was curious but cautious. He wanted only to observe. Red Cloud appeared. The Westerners stood and greeted him with honor. Once pleasantries were exchanged, they sat. A single man rose and came forward to address Red Cloud.

"We have journeyed long," he said. "We have endured difficulties along the way. But this does not compare to the misery and misfortune our people are suffering. Said simply, we need your help. We have heard of your grand battles. So we have come to ask for your assistance in defeating a great evil."

"How can I help?" asked Red Cloud.

"The affliction of my people is caused by a band of giants," he said.

The emissary hesitated as the onlookers became hushed. He continued.

"They capture and kill us. We try to run but they pursue us.

We try to hide but they track and find us. Our numbers have diminished. We cannot stop them. They are too big and too strong. Please help us, we have no place else to turn."

The Westerners became saddened. They hung their heads. A tear was seen in the eye of the emissary.

"Stop this evil. Free my people. I implore you good Chief," he said.

Red Cloud was moved. He glanced out across the gathering. He searched for the green eyes of his friend. His look met Quaid's. He saw the determination on his brother's face as Quaid nodded.

"We will help'" said Red Cloud. "We will find this evil and force it out. This I promise you."

There was a great rejoicing around the camp for the next few days. Spring is a time of revelry. It brings leaves that fly like festival flags. The flowers bloom in red, white, and violet. The birds sing. The bees buzz. All the animals of the earth come out to bathe in the shining light. They gorge themselves on the fresh food of the forest. They play in God's backyard. In Quaid's world all was well. But Red Cloud was somewhat subdued. He went to look for Quaid.

"Brother," started Red Cloud. " I must speak to you."

"About what?" asked Quaid.

"The pledge I have made," replied Red Cloud. "How can I order my warriors to go to a far away land and fight?"

"' A righteous man falling down before the wicked is as a troubled fountain, and a corrupt spring,'" quoted Quaid. (Proverbs 25:26).

"For me, I see it," said Red Cloud. "But for you, and for them?"

"As always, I am with you. So will your warriors be. Make it a request and not a command." said Quaid.

Red Cloud called for five volunteers to make the sacrifice. Five warriors came forward. A total of twelve made plans, packed supplies, and had their horses fed and watered. They said their goodbyes. A feast was held. Then, nighttime fell.

The pink hues of daybreak gave a feeling of calm to the troop. The rose-colored sky made the clouds blush. The yellow burning ball came up through the vast coral expanse. It was as a great apricot appearing in the air.

Red Cloud led out the pack. Quaid was right at his side. The remaining warriors followed. The Westerners traveled in the distance. The company moved slow at first. They passed under layers of tall trees and canopies. They climbed hills filled with cumulus green puffs of brush. They trailed through cirrus webs of spiders and stratified nests of insects. They ascended up into the infinite blue sky.

At a mark halfway past the caravan's path, the days began to run together. The company reached a mountain pass. There, they met with falling temperatures. The emissary of the Westerners took to the front. He guided the men over the elevation in the safest fashion. The pathfinder led the warriors up the peak as frozen teardrops fell from the sky. It was like a billion shooting stars coming down. Everywhere was white. The leaves, the trees, the bushes, and the grass were all covered in a frosting of pearl. The turf was hard. The air was harder. Gales blew gusts of glacial ice into their faces. The cold cut through their clothing, leaving them numb. Each took their turn out front, as the other went back behind the protected line of men riding in the driven wind. Intolerable levels were reached. They stopped and looked for shelter.

Quaid instructed the warriors to build three great fires in a triangular formation. The men stacked the wood high. Once lit, the frozen travelers stepped inside the glowing radiance away from the permafrost. The geometry gave a feeling of warmth all around. As his fingers thawed, Quaid's chilled mood melted. The men delighted in the amiable ambience. They ate and they slept. Quaid, Red Cloud, the warriors, and the Westerners stayed alive.

Going down the mountain gave relief. A wonderful feeling of comfort came to them. But as they moved further west, the heat escalated. The days of bright sun boiled them in a stew of their own juices. They stopped for any kind of shade. And even more frequently, they stopped for water. The air was dry and the horses were wet. Steadily they went. After all the weeks of difficult weather, they came to their destination, the southwest.

Red rocks jutted up from splashes of green and oceans of sand. The colored clay baked in the heat of the day. The wind blew the terra-cotta grains everywhere. It stuck to their skin like tar. The company moved through the maroon asphalt as hot stellar rays plastered the dust onto them. Mountainous wonders of ruby rock formed elevated peaks in the sky. Quaid noticed a small bluff that looked over the basin. Its ridge hung from the face as an old man's nose. Quaid pulled back on the reins of his horse and signaled Red Cloud.

"Up there!" shouted Quaid. "You can get a view of the entire valley."

Red Cloud nodded.

"We need to establish the topography of the area to get a plan of attack," continued Quaid.

"Agreed," yelled Red Cloud. "The warriors and I will remain hidden while you get a lay of the land."

Quaid dismounted. He tied his horse under some shade. He climbed the side of the cliff with skill. He scaled the crag as a spider would cross its web. He reached the top. From there, he waved to Red Cloud. Quaid walked to the ledge and lay flat. He pulled a pair a field glasses from his pack. The telescoping lenses allowed him to survey the canyon. He saw several caves carved into the earth. It transformed the wall of stone into a dark honeycomb. Some of the surrounding foliage obscured his view of the inhabitants. Beyond the entrances Quaid saw an open plain. He adjusted the glass into focus. He saw two large iron cauldrons simmering above immense fires. The pots were black and bubbling. An inferno raged underneath each of them. Quaid scanned the hollow. He saw multiple spikes sticking up from the ground. The pikes were at varying levels and intervals. Some reached eight feet into the air. To his horror, Quaid saw an atrocity like no other. It was men and women alive and impaled on the rods. Many were moving in their anguish. Pools of blood formed below their feet as they fought for life. Some were disemboweled. Some were dead. Some had separated limbs pinned next to their heads. Quaid sat back from the edge for a moment. He knew death, but this barbaric scene scorched his mind's eye. He turned back. Out from a cave came a pale white figure. The thing was huge. Its physical features were distorted. Its silvery skin was covered in bulbous irruptions. Its long red hair was stringy and damp. Its eyes were black. Out came another. These malformed beasts were massive. They towered over their captives. In disbelief, Quaid watched the giants move and work.

To the west, Quaid saw a big body of water. Several small ships made of reeds were at its shore. He would need to keep any assault between the lake and the caves to prevent a possible escape. The two giants came upon the cauldrons. One reached over the brim and pulled out a skewer. On the stick was a human leg. The giant held up the peg with his mouth open and sank his sharp teeth into the flesh. The razors tore at the tissue. He masticated the remains. As he chewed, drippings of blood drained from his mouth. The animal swallowed and repeated. He only stopped to spit the sinew from his craw. The grotesque cannibal fed as Quaid viewed the accursed sight.

Quaid climbed down from his perch. At the bottom, Red Cloud saw the distress on his brother's face.

"What is it?" asked Red Cloud.

"I am going in now," said Quaid firmly.

"Wait," said Red Cloud.

"I will take out as many as I can," said Quaid. "When you hear my signal come riding in."

"What signal?" asked Red Cloud.

"The sound of gunfire," said Quaid.

Quaid ran. He did not wait for a debate.

"How many are there?" asked Red Cloud.

Quaid was already out of earshot. Red Cloud readied his warriors. He nimbly traced Quaid's steps. An expert woodsman, Red Cloud concealed his whereabouts and advanced with stealth. Closer and closer the warriors came to the compound. They remained hidden. Red Cloud peered from under the cover and saw Quaid making his way to the settlement.

Quaid ran next to the shallow trenches that carried the blood of the impaled victims. He moved unnoticed along the ditch. Once in range, he released a single blade. The knife split the neck of a giant. The blood gushed out like a waterspout. It sprayed onto the other like the juice of an orange. Quaid threw another blade. It hit the second giant in the chest with a thud. The two dropped dead. A third giant came at him from the side. Quaid pulled out both Bowie knives and advanced in an angled attack. He struck the ogre down with a single slashing strike. The giant gave out a shriek. It broke the silence. The situation suddenly got chaotic. A dozen giants came clamoring from the caves with spears and swords. The behemoths charged at him. Quaid ran up the embankment to the massive pots of boiling remains. He grabbed a log from the fire and ignited a flame on the floating rendered fat. He kicked over the grease fire, sending a wave of incineration down upon the demons. In the molten madness, Quaid pulled out his revolver and began unloading its chambers. Bang! Bang! Bang! Red Cloud heard the gunshots. He turned to his warriors and shouted. "Go!" The cavalry rushed in. Red Cloud ran point. Archers let fly their arrows from their bows. They released dart after dart. Many giants dropped from the fury of the flying daggers. But the creatures kept coming. A berserker crashed into the side of one warrior's horse. It flung him to the ground. With a swing of a club, the colossus crushed the warrior. The battle raged. More giants streamed out of the caves like ants. Quaid continued to fire. He squeezed off shot after shot in rapid succession. The giants continued to rampage through the flames.

From a central cavern, through a wall of glowing gas, came an even larger giant. He glared at Quaid.

"Worm!" he shouted. "Face me! I am a god!"

"There is only one God," cried Quaid.

He had exhausted his rounds and could not fire. Quaid again readied his Bowie knives. The giant raised an enormous battle axe and gave him a sinful smile. Quaid saw the axe was made of sharpened steel wrapped in a wooden handle. Its two crescent-shaped sides were symmetric. It was dark and angular, with a keen taper.

"I will cut you down and swallow you whole!" boasted the giant.

"Try then," said Quaid.

The giant came hard at Quaid. He released a roundhouse swing of the axe. Quaid blocked the strike. One Bowie flew from his hand, so he countered with a sweep of the opposite pike. It was clipped easily by the giant. Quaid punched the beast. He landed a big body blow. But the slug had no effect. The giant smiled as he smacked Quaid back and off his feet with one arm. His jaw went numb. Quaid got up and shook out the cobwebs.

"You are no match for me," said the giant.

"My God is," said Quaid picking up his knives.

"I am god!" he screamed.

The giant raised his axe in anger. Quaid crossed his two blades above his head as the giant slammed the steel down against them. He held firm. The giant groaned as he increased the assailing force. Quaid pushed back on the pressure with all his might. His muscles began to twitch under the tension. The giant's great strength pushed Quaid in the reverse. He began to slide. Red Cloud saw the struggle. The giant moved Quaid steadily toward the fire. Red Cloud let go of an arrow with accuracy. It slit through the giant's Achilles tendon, bringing him down. His attack was broken off. Quaid instantly shoved the knives into his body. The blow sliced into his heart. The giant screamed and fell dead.

Quaid looked around. The casualties were high. All the warriors had been killed except for Red Cloud and himself. The lifeless figures lay scattered in pools of scarlet. The fires had stalled. Quaid and Red Cloud carried the bodies to the openings of the caves, and set them ablaze. The rise of the pyre cremated the remains. Quaid took a torch to the lake and he burned every reed boat.

"It is done," said Quaid to Red Cloud.

"It is done. But is it over?" asked Red Cloud.

"For now," replied Quaid. "Let us hope the remaining nations of the west can live in peace."

FIVE

The two warriors made their way eastward. The campaign had been long, and the price was high. Red Cloud and Quaid were exhausted. They barely spoke throughout the days of travel. They hardly slept the nights they tarried. They scarcely ate. Past events played over and over in their minds until even the numbness dulled. They were two ghost riders. One was a desolate spirit and the other a spectre. They had phased into shadows. Every apparition had faded into phantasm. It was the disillusion that death brings. The two trodded on only in faith. All that remained was the belief that God would bring back balance. The crusaders needed to find peace. Fidelity in their family and the familiar brought them home.

A short ride over the rise of a grassy knoll lay the valley of Red Cloud's people. At the top of the highland, Quaid brought his horse to a stop. He turned and talked to Red Cloud.

"Brother," said Quaid. " I cannot go further."

"Why?" asked Red Cloud.

"The valley is your home," said Quaid.

"It is your home too, brother," said Red Cloud.

"No it is not," said Quaid. "You are my brother, but the valley is not my home."

Quaid steadied his restless horse. He sat up high in the saddle.

"I still have a mother and a brother out there. I need to know if they are well. You are the leader of your people. You are their guide. I am a servant. They do not need me," said Quaid.

"I need you," said Red Cloud.

Quaid moved closer to Red Cloud by executing a side pass.

"And I will always need you, my friend," said Quaid. "But for now, I cannot stay."

Red Cloud remained steady as he contemplated a life without his friend.

"You will be missed," he said.

"I would hope so," said Quaid grinning.

Quaid rode off. As he did, Red Cloud called out. "Go with God brother! "

Quaid drove his horse east against the shining sun. He rode when he could. He rested when convenient. He ate when necessary. Quaid tracked back to his birthplace. He thought of what he might find in that one western town. He wondered how his mother had held up. He wondered how his brother grew up. Quaid felt a wave of guilt roll over him as he recalled when he left his baby brother behind. He felt that he had left for good reasons. But he felt that staying for his brother's welfare could have been a better one. Quaid was determined to face his family's afflictions. He wanted to ride in and right the wrongs.

Quaid arrived just after midday. He looked up at the house that held his childhood. He tied his horse loosely to a post. Quaid climbed the front steps slowly. He refused to knock on the door of his own home so he went inside.

"Mother!" he cried.

No answer came.

"It is Matthan!" he shouted.

All was quiet. Quaid glanced into the sitting room. It was empty. Both the dining and family rooms were vacant. He strode down the hall to the kitchen. It was bare. He proceeded to the bedroom in the back. The door was ajar. He pushed it open. There he saw an old woman laying in bed.

"Mom?" inquired Quaid.

He approached. He saw the thin covers rising and falling. She was sleeping. He sat down on the edge of the bed softly. He placed his hand on her shoulder. He felt the fragile flesh covering bone. He gave her a gentle jiggle.

"Mom," he said.

The old woman opened her eyes.

"Matty?" she asked.

"Yes, Mom," he said. "It is me."

"Oh my son," she said with great joy. "You came back to me."

"Of course," said Quaid. " I had to see you."

The old woman reached out to hug her son. He put his arms around her and drew her towards him.

"Where is Dad?" he asked.

"He died shortly after you left," said his mother.

Quaid let go of his grip and processed the implications of her words.

"And Robert?" he asked.

"Your brother moved east years ago," she said. "He is a pastor."

Quaid stood. He started to pace.

"Is he healthy and happy?" he asked.

"I believe so," replied his mother.

Quaid stopped. He was comforted by the news. He sat down next to his mother again.

"Why are you in bed in the middle of the day?" he asked.

"I am just a little tired," she said. His mother stared right through him. She seemed confused. "Are you real?" she asked.

"Yes Mom," said Quaid. " I am very real."

"Good," she said happily. "Go get settled. I will fix your favorite breakfast in the morning."

"Okay Mom," said Quaid. "Just rest."

Quaid walked toward the door. He turned and regarded his aged mother. She seemed to almost disappear beneath the blankets. Quaid smiled as he shut the door slowly. He remembered when the roles were reversed. He remembered when he was the one snuggled under the covers. And it was his mother who peeked through the shrinking crack as it closed.

Quaid went outside to feed and water his horse. He took the animal to the barn. Afterward, he settled the other animals on the farm. Quaid retired to his old room. It had shrunk. The color was the same but the accessories had changed. It was of no matter now, he was tired. He would explore more tomorrow. He lay his large frame on top of the tiny bunk. Soon, he was asleep.

A light came streaming through the door. It was bright white. The reflected haze obscured what was beyond. Quaid raised his hand over his eyes. It gave little help. He got up and moved toward the opening. As he approached the portal, a hill of tall grass came into focus. It was a gorgeous green with speckles of purple flowers around its base. Upon its crown, he saw two trees. One was tall with Kelly colored leaves. It was in the shape of a spade, pointing upward. The bottom was wide and rounded. It was the picture of a robust and beautiful arbor. The second tree was stripped to its core. There were no leaves and no bark. The wood was a pale shade of grey. Its branches looked like broken bones. They were bent and disjointed. It stood like a symbol of a state beyond death. Quaid saw a young woman climbing the hill. She carried a metal watering can. She doused the full tree. It immediately became greener. The woman turned and faced him. It was his mother. She poured a stream of water over the second tree. It erupted into flames. The fire consumed the boughs. Quaid felt the flash of heat. He woke with the sun's rays radiating across his face. He leapt to his feet. He headed directly to his mother's room and threw open the door.

"Mom!" he shouted.

Looking down, he saw no movement.

"Mom!" he shouted again.

He hoped to wake her from her slumber. The room was oddly still. He moved closer to the bed. Gently, he placed his hand on her arm. It was rigid. She was cold. Quaid sat as he realized what had happened.

"Oh Mom," he let out sadly.

Quaid hung his head. He remained motionless. Sorrow and regret steeped into his spirit. A tear formed as he was flooded by emotion. He gasped in despondent melancholy.

"No," he whispered.

Quaid buried his mother in the cemetery where his father had been laid to rest so many years before. A good crowd gathered around the grave. They were members from church and friends from town. Quaid stood alone near the headstone. It was near the pastor's left. During the dedication, he stared deeply into the opening in the ground.

"'Let not your heart be troubled. Ye believe in God, believe also in me. In my Father's house are many mansions. If it were not so, I would have told you. I go to prepare a place for you,'" said the pastor. (John 14:1-2).

He blessed the burial. Closing his Bible, he walked over to the stoic son.

"I am sorry," he said.

"Thank you," said Quaid.

The pastor saw the angst on his face. He addressed him.

"'Grace be to you and peace from God our Father and from the Lord Jesus Christ. Blessed be God, even the Father of our Lord Jesus Christ, the Father of mercies, and God of all comfort; Who comforteth us in all our tribulation,'" he said. (2 Cor 1:2-4).

"Thanks for those kind words," said Quaid.

"Your mother will be missed," said the pastor.

"She is already missed," said Quaid.

He moved away from the gravesite and walked toward the cemetery's entrance. The pastor watched as the sullen figure disappeared like a flickering candle. Quaid returned to the ranch. It was more empty than it had ever been. The house was no longer a home. He didn't recognize any of the doors, halls, or rooms. It was an enigmatic maze without an exit. He felt trapped. Reluctantly, Quaid retired to his room. He had difficulty sleeping. His sadness stoked the insomnia. He tossed and turned throughout the night. The more he tried to rest, the worse his restlessness became. Finally, he fell into a deep sleep.

Quaid found himself standing in front of a towering estate. It was white with Corinthian pillars that went up farther than he could see. Double doors of glimmering silver stood wide open. He walked in. He saw a great hall with stairs leading to levels upon levels. He saw floors and doors everywhere. Quaid climbed the first set of stairs. He came upon a glass gate. It was unfastened. He pushed on the crystalline entrance. As he did, Quaid heard a familiar voice.

"Come in son," said his mother's voice.

"Mom?" he questioned. "What are you doing here?"

"There are many rooms," she said.

"What?" asked Quaid.

His mother pointed up and to the right. "Your room," she said.

Quaid walked over to a long landing with risers. A giant chamber rose from above his head. The walls began to expand and grow. They kept increasing until he could no longer see its end. His heart fell from his chest.

"This is for me?" he asked.

"Yes," replied his mother.

Quaid ascended higher. The room was vast. Transparent walls circled around him like a warm breeze. It created a kind of cavernous cocoon. He was overcome by the grandeur.

Quaid awoke in the small space of his earthly home. He sat up in bed. A feeling of serenity replaced the anxiety of loss. He made his way to his mother's room. The bed was made. Everything was tidy and clean. He looked all around. His eye stopped at the nightstand. Next to the lamp sat a small Bible. He picked it up. Quaid opened it at its bookmark. He read.

"'Jesus said unto her, I am the resurrection, and the life. He that believeth in me, though he were dead, yet shall he live.'" he murmured. (John 11:25).

Quaid smiled in memory of his mother. He took the book and went to get dressed.

Quaid went to church. It was the church of his family. The church was a simple structure. It was made of painted white wood. It had a single steeple dressed in black trim. The double door was flanked by windows on each side. The interior was a rectangle. Unimaginative pews filled the space. Quaid walked into the empty sanctuary. The sound of his footsteps striking the floor echoed. He continued past the altar to the rear of the church and went down a narrow hallway. It guided him to the pastor's office.

"Come in," said the pastor.

Quaid entered the room and saw the clergyman sitting behind a large desk.

"Please, have a seat," he said. "What can I do for you?"

Quaid sat.

"I came to ask about my brother, Robert," said Quaid.

"Yes?" inquired the pastor.

"You knew him well?" asked Quaid.

"I did," he replied.

"Where is he now?" asked Quaid.

"Robert entered the seminary back east where he became a pastor," he replied.

"Where back east?" asked Quaid.

"Philadelphia," replied the pastor. " I can give you the address."

The pastor opened the top drawer of the desk and pulled out a sheet of writing paper. He reached forward and grabbed a container of ink. With a pen, he scribbled onto the page. Once it dried, he handed it to Quaid.

"Thank you," said Quaid.

"City of Brotherly Love," said the pastor smiling.

"I suppose," said Quaid on his way out.

Quaid packed his saddlebags and readied his horse for the excursion across country. Before leaving, he placed his mother's pocket Bible into the front of his vest. He rode east with an ease about himself. He was in no hurry. He took in every mountain, stream, and tree. He counted each cloud. Quaid took time to lay in the shade. He bathed in the blue sky. He filled his lungs with life. He catalogued the beauty of God's great earth.

Quaid arrived in Philadelphia early in the day. He took out the slip of paper with the location of his brother's church. He reviewed the address. Quaid continued to the center of town. There, he entered into an area heavily trafficked by pedestrians. He got off his horse and walked. Quaid looked for signs and numbers to help guide him on his way. The city was large. To a man of the wilderness it was confusing. He came upon a clothing store. He tied off his ride and went inside.

"Hello," said the shopkeeper. "My name is Carl. Carl Howe. What can I help you with, sir?"

"I need some information," said Quaid.

"Information on a shirt or slacks?" he asked.

"I am looking for a church," said Quaid. He pulled out the scrap of paper and showed it to the shopkeeper. "Do you know how to get here?" asked Quaid.

"Sure," said Carl. " I know that church."

He came out from behind the counter and walked to the door. Carl opened it and stepped out. Quaid followed. On the street the shopkeeper began to point.

"Go three blocks down. Then you need to turn left," he said. "Go two more blocks and you will see it there."

"Thank you, Carl," said Quaid.

"My pleasure," he replied. "And if you ever decide to update that outfit, please, come back."

"I will," said Quaid. "And thanks again."

Quaid followed the shopkeeper's directions. Soon he found himself standing in front of an old stone church. He made his way up the brick path. The masonry he walked on matched the cardinal color of the front door. The crimson walkway took him through a small cemetery. There were graves on either side. There were large and small headstones. They were upright and flat, singular and side-by-side. The chapel rock was a grey-brown color. There were two rectangular windows above the door. One was slightly smaller than the other. Both were trimmed in white. The steeple was an equally alabaster hue. The entrance underneath was tall and thin. It looked like a red rocket. Behind that was a square structure, covered in shingles.

Quaid entered. The walls of the sanctuary were a soft cream. The ambient light of the stained glass windows added color to the ivory pews. It took only a few steps to get to the pulpit. From the back of the podium came a man in a robe. He walked up and met Quaid where he stood.

"Service is not for several hours," he said.

"I am looking for Robert," said Quaid.

"Just around there and to the right," he said. "He is taking confession."

"Thank you," said Quaid politely.

He walked around the corner. He opened the box door and sat down on the shriving seat.

"Forgive me, for I have sinned," began Quaid.

"What was your sin?" the question came.

"It is not what I did," replied Quaid. "It was what I did not do."

There was a short silence.

"What did you, not, do then?" he asked.

Quaid swallowed hard after hearing his brother's voice from the other side.

"I failed my family," said Quaid. "You see, my father had taken to drink. He became a different person under its influence. I tried to honor my father as the Bible directs. But I became weary of his cruelty, so I left home. I went and left my mother and baby brother behind. At the time, I believed it was being reverent to God."

"And now you do not?" asked his brother.

"No," replied Quaid. " I should have stayed to protect my mother and brother. Instead I ran. I left them alone in their difficulty."

"Was this recent?" asked his brother.

"I was a boy at the time," said Quaid.

"You were young, and it was a long time ago," said his brother. "You should not blame yourself."

"But I do," said Quaid sadly.

"Your brother and your mother, are they well?" he asked.

"My mother has passed," replied Quaid. " I only want to confess my wrong and tell my brother that I am sorry."

"I am sure he will accept your apology," he said.

There was a long pause.

"Then, please, forgive me brother," said Quaid.

He heard the door of the confessional burst open. He stepped out and saw Robert. Tears of joy fell from Robert's cheek to the corner of his smile. His arms were outstretched as he moved towards Quaid. Robert grabbed his brother and did not let go.

"Matthan!" he exclaimed. "Come with me," said Robert as he released his hold. "You must be tired and thirsty from your trip."

Quaid accompanied his brother to the diaconicon of the chapel. Robert opened the door to a world of books, vestments, and artifacts. Quaid looked over the living library. He saw his young brother had attained the wisdom of a much older man. He felt a strong pride well up inside. He began to smile.

"Have a seat, we have much to talk about," said Robert. "And tell me everything."

"It is a long story. Even longer since mother has prohibited the use of contractions," Quaid said in a laugh.

"No cursing. No contractions," the two men said in unison, mocking their mother.

Robert chuckled. "She was always so formal," he said.

They talked and they talked. And then they talked some more. Quaid remained in Philadelphia with his brother. They ventured out into the city together. The brothers frequented the theaters and toured the museums. They experienced fine dining. Pages of the calendar turned. Quaid took to work. He rented a small living quarters not far from Robert's church. He went to Sunday service every week. He was a constant at Robert's sermons. He enjoyed every moment.

Week after week a member of the congregation caught Quaid's attention. His eye centered on a young girl. She was a classic beauty. Her heart shaped face was accentuated by high cheekbones. Her full lips turned up at the corners in a symmetrical fashion. She had caramel colored hair. The long strands of satin flowed like poured honey. Her eyes were balanced, round, and brown. She was delicate and her length was long. Her statuesque figure moved with a fluid motion that never went unnoticed by Quaid.

Robert saw his brother's attraction to the girl. He decided to make an introduction. Robert surprised him from behind. Quaid turned to see the young lady at Robert's side.

"Matthan, this is Beatrice," said Robert.

Quaid stood expressionless. Before he could conjure up a response, Robert continued. "Beatrice, this is my big brother, Matthan," he said.

The girl smiled widely at him. He felt his heart flash.

"It is nice to meet you," she said.

Quaid couldn't come up with a reply. So he just smiled. Seeing the uncomfortable exchange, Robert jumped back into the conversation.

"Brother, I have asked Beatrice to join us at the church picnic this afternoon. Is that not wonderful?" Robert asked.

"Yes," said Quaid softly.

"Great," said Robert. "And Beatrice, we look forward to seeing you later today."

"I do as well," she replied with a shy smile.

Time went by quickly, but not for Quaid. Robert went to check on his brother. He gave a firm knock on his door. Quaid opened it and Robert walked in. Quaid began to pace.

"What is on your mind?" asked Robert.

"The picnic," replied Quaid.

"Is it the picnic or the girl?" teased Robert.

Quaid stopped moving. He gave his brother a stare.

"I have nothing to wear," he said.

"I see," said Robert. "You never let that stop you from attending church."

"This is different," said Quaid.

"How so?" asked Robert pushing his brother's buttons.

"You know how," said Quaid a bit annoyed.

"Okay, okay," said Robert. "Let me talk to some of my parishioners. I am sure someone would be happy to loan you a suit and vest."

"Thank you brother," said Quaid. " I know a tailor but there is no time."

"I understand," said Robert with a heckling grin.

"Just for that you can add a top hat too," said Quaid as he pushed him out the door.

It was a beautiful day, warm and bright. At the side of the old stone church were layers of cloth-covered tables full of food. On the nearby grass was a patchwork of picnic blankets spread out all the way to the river. Large oaks and birch sprung from the ground. Elms hung over the water. Their wide expanse gave great shade for the diners below. The eclipsed light provided a cool shadow of protection. Many parishioners were found encircling the church. Volunteers dispensed food and drink. The ladies of the congregation were dressed mostly in white with high lace collars. The ivory enclosed their necks. The majority of the attire was monochrome but some dresses were two tones of blue. The lighter color was on top, and the darker on the bottom. A few ensembles had stripes. Most men were in brown or grey. Each man's wardrobe had a vest. A draped chain secured their gold timepieces into the small side pockets.

Quaid appeared in all black. He had a rounded bowler hat. His dark suit had no tie. There was just a tab collar. The pants were straight. His shoes were spit-shined leather. And they looked it. Robert walked over to his brother. He gave him a strong slap on the back.

"Very nice," he said.

"I look like an undertaker," said Quaid.

"That is because your clothes come from a furniture maker," said Robert laughing.

Quaid was not happy. Robert saw the distaste on his face.

"Sorry, I could not help myself," said Robert. " I thought a little levity would lighten the mood."

"Forgive me if I bury my laughter," said Quaid sternly.

"You are dressed for it," said Robert joking.

Quaid groaned.

"Go grab some food," continued Robert. "Find a nice spot to sit. Relax and enjoy yourself. Be happy, brother."

Quaid glanced over to the serving area. There were picnickers of different sizes and shapes squeezing into line. The jigsaw puzzle of people was more social interaction than Quaid desired. Robert noticed his hesitation.

"Brother," said Robert. "Why not go down to that tree over there and I will bring you something to eat."

Quaid looked towards the riverbank. There he saw a mushroom shaped Elm tree drinking from the shoreline. Underneath there was a large white quilt covering the thick grass. Seated daintily on bent knee in a blue gown was Beatrice. Her top was a deep navy color with interrupting white stripes. Her head was adorned by a refined raised hat with a low brim. In front was mounted a single red feather. It pointed skyward. She sat by herself gripping an umbrella with both hands. Quaid made his way forth. As he came upon her blanket, he removed his hat.

"Lovely day, is it not?" asked Quaid.

"Yes it is," replied Beatrice. "Are you to meet someone this day?"

"'I would I could find in my heart that I had not a hard heart. For truly I love none. '" said Quaid. (Shakespeare, Much Ado About Nothing, Act 1 Scene 1).

"'A dear happiness to women. They would else have been troubled with a pernicious suitor. I thank God and my cold blood, I am of your humour for that. I had rather hear my dog bark at a crow than a man swear he loves me.'" quoted Beatrice. (Shakespeare, Much Ado About Nothing, Act 1 Scene 1).

"'God keep your ladyship still in that mind!'" replied Quaid. (Shakespeare, Much Ado About Nothing, Act 1 Scene 1).

"I am flabbergasted, Mr. Quaid," said Beatrice.

"Why so?" asked Quaid.

"I was told you were a man of the wilderness, not a scholar," replied Beatrice.

"Miss Beatrice, I am no scholar. But I do like to read," he said smiling.

"And what about the stories of you killing giants?" she asked.

"A slight exaggeration of my loving brother, I am afraid," he replied.

"Slight exaggeration?" she questioned. "What's next? Maybe the slaying of a dragon?" she said in jest.

"For you, Miss Beatrice, I would," replied Quaid in delight.

"Please, Mr. Quaid, join me," said Beatrice.

"Call me Matthan," said Quaid.

Quaid bent his legs and lowered his large frame onto the quilt. He extended his feet forward and rested his forearms on his knees.

"You look stunning," he said.

"Thank you," said Beatrice.

There was a small silence.

"I like your suit," she said. "Very formal."

Quaid grinned. "It is the custom," he said. " I dug it out for today."

Beatrice laughed. Quaid leaned slightly in her direction.

"They are borrowed," he said.

"I hope from the living," said Beatrice chuckling.

"Yes, of course," said Quaid smiling greatly.

Beatrice took a minute to look him over from head to toe.

"In some strange way, it befits you," she said.

Quaid grabbed both lapels and adjusted his coat. " I agree," he said.

The two carried on a conversation for hours without interruption. Robert stopped by later with a couple plates of food.

"You looked hungry," said Robert.

"Thank you," said Beatrice.

Quaid took the plates from his brother. "Very kind of you," he said.

"Are you enjoying your day?" asked Robert with a prying tone.

Quaid refused to reply.

"I am having an exceedingly good day," said Beatrice jubilantly.

"Wonderful!" exclaimed Robert.

Quaid glared at Robert with a sour expression. But he held his tongue. He did not engage his brother but gazed joyfully back at Beatrice.

"So, are you having a good day brother?" asked Robert persistently.

"Yes," replied Quaid reluctantly.

"Great!" answered Robert. " I will leave you at present. I love you, brother."

"I love you too," replied Quaid halfheartedly.

Time marched on. The days stepped in double time. The night moved even faster. Weeks advanced into months. Beatrice became more attached to Quaid with each moment. He felt the same. Their time together created closeness. They became inseparable. They became a couple. All was good. It was better than good.

One early morning Quaid heard a loud rap at his door. He opened the egress. Robert quickly came through the entryway.

"Come in," said Quaid sarcastically.

"Close the door please," said Robert.

"What is this about?" asked Quaid.

"It is about you," said Robert in a troubled tone. Robert looked at his brother in wonderment. He continued. "The city's Police Marshall came to see me last night."

"Police Marshall?" asked Quaid.

"He is the top law enforcement official here in Philadelphia," replied Robert.

"The sheriff?" asked Quaid.

"This is a city of half a million people. We have a large number of men that work for law enforcement. This is not the wild west," said Robert.

"Okay," said Quaid in an attempt to calm his brother.

"The Police Marshall is looking for a man involved in a street fight last night," said a nervous Robert. " I think it was you."

"And?" questioned Quaid.

"And?... You put eight men in the hospital," replied Robert angrily.

"It felt more like four," replied Quaid in jest.

"This is no joke," replied Robert sternly.

"Look, I do not have to explain defending myself to anyone. Not even you," said Quaid bluntly.

"Maybe not me, but you will have to explain it to the Marshall if he finds you," said Robert.

"Doubt he will discover me in a city of... What did you say, a half million people," said Quaid.

Quaid's arms hung from his side. Robert looked down at his hands. He reached out and clasped Quaid's left wrist. He turned the palm over revealing the sign of the cross.

"One of the men described the unique mark on your hand. The Marshall is searching places of worship for a man with this brand," said Robert.

Quaid walked into the next room and sat down. Robert followed. He placed himself directly across from his brother.

"I had just taken Beatrice home," said Quaid. " I went inside for only a few minutes. When I came out my horse was gone. He had been stolen. I tracked the thieves to the wharf. I found my horse at the stockyard. A gang of eight men were there, laughing and joking. I approached them and asked for his return. Their leader refused. He said that the horse was not my property. He said it was his horse. To prove it, he shot and killed the animal. So, I punished them," said Quaid.

"I get it," said Robert. "But punishing criminals is not your job."

"What would you have me do? They killed my horse!" exclaimed Quaid.

"Walk away, or go to get the police," replied Robert firmly.

"I am done running. Remember?" stated Quaid forcefully.

"This is not about that," said Robert. "This is not about you and me."

"I will not run," replied Quaid sternly.

Robert stood and walked briskly to the door. He twisted the knob and stepped out. Quaid got up and followed him. Robert faced him.

"Tell that to Beatrice," said Robert. He looked into Quaid's eyes of green. Robert pulled a pair of black gloves from under his belt and threw them at him.

"And cover that up," he said.

The gloves hit Quaid in the chest. They fell separately to the ground. One landed inside the residence and the other did not. Quaid ignored them and slammed the door shut. He carried his six foot four inch frame into the parlor and crashed it into his chair. He fumed. Quaid was offended by his brother's words. What kind of representative of God can Robert be to deny justice, he thought. He stewed. Quaid went to his bedroom. He decided to pray about it. He quieted his soul, and got down on his knees.

"'Show me Your ways, O Lord. Teach me thy paths. Lead me in Your truth and teach me, for thou art the God of my salvation,'" prayed Quaid. (Psm 25:4-5).

At once the spirit moved him. He felt an overwhelming need to protect his family, both Robert and Beatrice. He decided to go back to the place he fit in best, the west. He prepared a light pack and headed for the door. As he readied to leave, Quaid stepped on a lump of leather. Looking down, he saw a solitary glove. He picked it up and placed it on his left hand. It covered the cross. He went directly to Beatrice's residence. Quaid knocked on the door and she appeared.

"Hello," she said happily.

"Bea," said Quaid. " I need to tell you something."

"Would you like to come in?" she asked.

"No, thank you," replied Quaid. "You see, I have to leave."

"Why?" asked Beatrice.

"Because of something I did," said Quaid. " I must go."

"I don't understand," said Beatrice.

"I am sorry, Bea," he said. "But I am traveling back west."

"Wait," said Beatrice. " I will go with you."

"It is not safe," said Quaid.

"I have never felt more safe than when I am with you," she said.

"What about your life here?" asked Quaid.

"You are my life," she replied.

Quaid nodded and smiled. "Very well," he said.

He stepped inside and Beatrice began to collect her things.

"Bea," he yelled from the front room. " I lost my horse. We have no means to move west."

"We will take the iron horse then," she replied.

Beatrice came forward carrying a bag made of thick cloth. She wore a suit of brown with matching slacks. A wide leather belt circled her waist. On her head was a rounded hat with a large extended brim.

"I am ready," she said.

"That was fast," said Quaid.

"Let's go," she said.

Quaid hugged her. "When we arrive, we will marry," he said.

"I accept," said Beatrice smiling.

The two took the train to Chicago. It was a long ride but pleasant. The passing scenery was beautiful. They sat and relaxed. They enjoyed the trip. From Chicago the two took a steamboat south. Upon arrival, Quaid moved Beatrice into his family home. They married. Their first child came right away. It was a boy. They named him Jacob.

Quaid worked the ranch. He planted crops. He acquired horses, cattle, and chickens. They thrived on the farm. Quaid took his goods into the city often to be sold. He and Beatrice became part of the community.

Quaid's chores again took him back into town. He hitched his wagon up near the jailhouse. He walked to the bank. He stopped at the general store. Quaid purchased the packaged goods his wife needed. As he walked the wooden planks of the storefronts, he glanced into the windows.

In the street, a strange scene caught Quaid's eye. He saw two men in a flatbed pulling a black man behind it with a rope. The sight of him being treated like cattle disturbed Quaid. He moved directly to them. With a strong arm, he grabbed the reins of the team and help them fast.

"What's wrong with you Mister!" screamed the driver.

Quaid walked to the passenger side. There, sat an unshaven cowboy. The wrangler had a shotgun sitting across his lap. Quaid looked them over. He leaned back and glanced at the prisoner being towed.

"Are you okay?" Quaid asked the captive.

"Don't talk to my property, Mister!" the driver shouted.

"Property?" questioned Quaid. "He does not look like a cow to me."

The cowboy pointed the barrels of his gun at him. Quaid snatched the weapon from his hand. He threw the cowboy off the rig into the dust. The man landed hard.

"This is a free state," said Quaid. "So he is a free man."

"The law says I can come and get my property, free state or not," said the driver.

He dropped the reins and reached for his pistol. Quaid climbed onto the backboard. He seized the driver by the collar and tossed him like pitching hay. The cowboy landed next to his partner. Quaid went to the back and began to untie the slave's bonds.

"Matthan!" shouted a loud voice. "You can't do this!"

Quaid stopped for a second. He looked up to see the town's sheriff approaching.

"The law is on their side," said the sheriff.

"I do not care about man's laws," replied Quaid.

He started to unravel the rope again.

"Matthan stop! I won't let you do this," said the sheriff.

"You know this is wrong!" yelled Quaid.

"It doesn't matter," said the sheriff. "It is the law."

"Right and wrong always matter," said Quaid.

"I don't like it either," said the sheriff. "But I'm sworn to uphold the law."

The slave owners got to their feet.

"Arrest that man!" the driver shouted.

"He can't do this!" the second shouted.

"Shut up!" bellowed the sheriff.

He walked halfway to the back of the hitch.

"Matthan, it's not the right time or place," he said.

"Then when?" asked Quaid.

The sheriff went right up to him. " I knew your mother. I know Bea and Jake. End this, for their sake," he said.

Quaid relented. He gave a vengeful stare to the cowboys and moved off.

"Aren't you taking him in?" asked the driver.

"Sorry boys," said the sheriff. "Nobody wins today."

Quaid went to his wagon. He directed his horse towards home.

"Hold on," shouted the sheriff from behind.

"What?" answered Quaid fuming.

"I understand, Matthan," said the sheriff.

"I think not," replied Quaid. "Or you would not have stopped me."

"If you really want change, then volunteer," said the sheriff. "The Union needs good fighting men."

Quaid turned away and drove off.

SIX

March 17,1862

My Dearest Beloved,

It is evening. I am finally able to sit and write. Dearest, I wish to see your shining face. I wish I could hold you in my arms and watch as the sun dips below the horizon. I wish to kiss you gently on the cheek. As it is, I must simply imagine your beauty as the twilight twinkles in your eyes. The pain of the day's onerous march is only matched by the suffering my heart endures being far from your love, our home, and our son. I dream of the day I shall return to you. I have not yet fired a single shot, but without you at my side I am already warworn. I have never relished battle. Yet, I would surely fight a million men to be back in the warmth of your embrace, my Beloved. At present it feels like I am the sun, chasing the moon around and around the earth again and again, never to meet. My Dearest, know that I will not stop reaching for you, not even into the heavens. I will see our sweet rendezvous come true. My Darling, do not be troubled. My heart carries enough love for both of us. I will return to you soon.

Our company came by steamboat down the Tennessee River to arrive at Pittsburg Landing. The spring rains have been a real toad strangler. It made for a long hike, interrupted by swollen creeks and tributaries. Our progress was blocked. We were forced to pace back to the transport. The boat steamed farther making ground at the base of the landing. The men and I disembarked and were paraded south. Our camp is near a creek, next to a small grove of peach trees. Our commander, General Sherman, is two miles along the line to the west. Our boys are nestled between the fifty-fourth and the seventy-first Ohio regimens. As I draft this letter, I am sitting outside my tent by the fire. I am enjoying a cup of hot coffee. I always carry a handful of beans in my pocket though. It makes the long marchs easier. I dined on salt pork, molasses, and hard bread. I feel full. The boys around the camp are jubilant for being so tired.

General Sherman has not been by, but it is said we are to move south to Corinth from here. As you remember, he was in command at Benton Barracks in St. Louis. I was stationed there after training at Camp Douglas in Chicago. As I look around the camp, I see young boys who are very green and yet to experience death. They continue to drill, but nothing prepares you for the horror that comes with conflict. I empathize. But warm feelings will not stop a Minie ball. I pray that they will be ready for what comes next.

You will be happy to know that I made a friend. I generally keep to myself. I prefer being alone to large crowds. But I expect this young boy to be a true friend. I do sincerely believe he needed one. His name is Michael. He is a funny little guy. I call him Mikey. He is tiny and thin. He is so thin that I think a strong wind could carry him away. He is a meek man with blonde colored tufts of hair. His voice squeaks like a mouse, and it often cracks when he gets excited. Mikey is the son of a lawyer. He is definitely not built for war. Apparently his father had to impress his friends and associates by forcing his son to volunteer. He is terrified. I first encountered Mikey on the deck of our steamboat. He was wallpapered. Colonel Stuart confronted him about his drunkenness in front of the other men. Mikey insisted that he was only half drunk. The colonel rudely suggested he be fully intoxicated the next time. The boys made much fun of him after that. I felt moved to defend him. Mikey is merely fearful, and a boy. He is not a fighting man. And neither are most, I reminded the men. They are farmers, accountants, and such. All the men here carry the worry of war. Mikey let his dread of death get the best of him. Drink gives a man courage. Maybe too much courage. So now I have a new friend. Often times it feels more like having a new puppy. What I like about him is that he has a good heart.

My coffee grows cold my Beloved. I will place my pencil and paper down for now. Know that as I sleep, I will dream of your gentle touch. As I breathe, I inhale the flames of our love that burn everlasting. Good night my Sweet.

Yours Eternal,
Matthan

April 5,1862

My Dearest Beloved,

It is a grey and blue day. It rained so hard last night I slept on my weapons to keep them dry. I rose early this morning to the dreary dampness. Later, the sun came out. The clouds cleared, revealing a beautiful sapphire sky. The glowing rays gave me some comfort. Yet not as much as when I see you smile. Not even the sun's magnificent luminance warms me like you do. Most of the boys here believe the war will be over quickly. Something tells me that is not the case. A prolonged war will keep me from you for way too long. I think of home at all times. And I miss you every hour of every day. I am thankful to be healthy and well.

The boys have settled into camp life these past few weeks. It has been like one long picnic. It reminds me of our first day together by the fertile grounds of the church. That was a glorious time. Nowadays, we begin with discipline. We rise. We eat. We drill. By the afternoon the circumstances change from order to upheaval. The boys are good humored about it. They are just bored.

I went for a walk the other day. My friend, Mikey, went with me. He is such a strange fellow. Past the trees, there were pastures of grass and flowers. A bed of purple violets caught Mikey's eye. He ran over and lay down in the middle of them. He carefully picked a bouquet and placed petals around the brim of his hat. What a sight he was. I could not let the other soldiers see him play the fool. I scolded him and knocked the hat from his head. Tears came to his eyes. He said the violets symbolized peace. Then he told me he was afraid to fight. I understand that he is scared. He has never held a gun in his life until now. I feel for my friend. I vowed to protect him. He smiled and thanked me. My Beloved, I pray each day for his safety. My Love, when you pray for me I ask that you pray also for my friend. Yours is a kind heart. Mine has been made better by you. It beats only because of you. I look forward to the day when our hearts will be reunited. God bless you my Sweet.

Yours Eternal,
Matthan

Quaid woke before daybreak. He picked up his haversack and gun. As the morning star crawled out of bed, he headed north. Quaid made his way to the post office. Along the way, he found a secluded place to pray. He knelt.

"'Cause me to hear thy loving kindness in the morning for in thee do I trust. Cause me to know the way wherein I should walk, for I lift my soul into thee.'" prayed Quaid. (Psm 143:8)

After completing his devotion, Quaid continued northwest to the postal service tent. He reached into his pocket where he carried coffee beans. He plucked them out and chewed the hard brown berries as he walked. Quaid headed more west to cross the main road to the landing. Upon nearing the Hamburg-Savannah Road, he heard the sound of horses hooves and rolling wagon wheels. In the lifeless first light, it echoed in his ears like a cock's crow. Quaid stepped from the foliage to meet the transport.

"Hello!" shouted Quaid. "Are you going up to the landing?" he asked.

"Woah!" shouted the driver of the team. "Yes, we are going to the landing to load supplies," replied the driver.

"Can I hitch a ride?" asked Quaid.

"Hop on," came the reply.

There were two young boys sitting on the front buckboard. There was another reclined in the back. Quaid climbed in. He immediately noticed the clothing of his companions was grey in color.

"In what unit do you boys serve?" asked Quaid.

"We are in the ninth Illinois," said the driver. "Our colonel sent us to collect the regiment's Union blues. I guess we look a little like butternuts dressed like this."

"I am with the fifty-fifth Illinois," said Quaid. "My name is Matthan."

"I am Richard," said the driver. "And this is Darren," he said looking at his partner upfront. "That back there is Miller."

The boy nodded. Quaid looked the group over. All three were just kids. The trio grinned at Quaid in unison. The exaggerated smiles amplified their baby-faced cheeks.

"Where is your home town?" asked Quaid.

"Oh, we don't live in town," replied Richard. "We are from the farm."

"I milk cows," said Darren with enthusiasm.

"What about you, Miller?" asked Quaid.

The boy just stared at him.

"Don't mind Miller," said Richard. "He doesn't talk much."

Quaid sat back against the bench as they moved. He glanced

over at Miller. The boy just kept smiling. His look made Quaid uncomfortable. When the wagon reached the supply house, Quaid jumped off.

"Thanks for the lift boys," he said.

"You need a ride back?" asked Richard.

"No, thank you," said Quaid. "Besides, it is a nice morning. I think I will just walk."

Quaid walked down to the postal service tent. He dipped his head as he entered. The postmaster addressed him.

"Can I help you soldier?" he asked.

Quaid pulled a letter from his jacket pocket. He looked at the stamp affixed to the envelope.

"My last stamp," he said.

"Don't worry," said the postmaster. "You can simply write 'soldier's letter' on the envelope and rest assured, it will be delivered."

"Thank you," said Quaid handing him the letter.

"Certainly," the postmaster replied. "And it looks like it's going to be another great day too."

Quaid nodded and smiled. He exited the tent and made his way down to the landing. He wanted to take a look at the Union gunboats. He sat at the water's edge wondering how much longer it would be before he saw conflict. He wondered if these very young boys would be ready. They were beyond green.

Boom! Boom! Boom! Pop! Pop! Pop! Pop! Blasts of artillery fire rang from far off. Quaid immediately darted up the incline of the landing. The cannonade intensified as he reached the top. He looked around as mayhem sent men running in all directions. The barrage seemed to be emanating from the south and west. Quaid broke out into a full sprint in the direction of the shelling. The volleys were rapid. The explosions continued without interruption. Quaid ran down the Hamburg road. Dust kicked up behind him. He desperately needed to get to his company.

In the distance, Quaid saw the boys of the ninth Illinois on the ground. Their wagon had overturned. He ran to their location.

Quaid worried about the boys. As he got closer, he saw that everyone appeared to be alive and unharmed. He ran right up to them.

"Is everyone all right?" inquired Quaid.

"I think so," said Richard.

Quaid helped the boys turn the wagon upright. Darren held the horses steady as Quaid and Richard checked the harnesses. Miller began picking up the uniforms and supplies. The sounds of battle seemed to come closer.

"Maybe you boys should get into those uniforms before someone mistakes you for the enemy," said Quaid.

"Good idea," said Richard.

As Miller removed his coat Quaid grabbed it from him.

"Miller," said Quaid. "Climb that tree over there and look for the Rebel's position."

"What?" asked Miller.

"Go now!" commanded Quaid. "Before I kick you up to the top!"

"Okay, okay," said Miller.

"Richard, Darren," said Quaid. "Load your muskets now. And have a reload ready."

Richard and Darren went immediately to work. They fixed several muskets and laid them in the back of the wagon. Quaid walked to the edge of the woods. He looked up to see Miller making his way up the tree.

"Where is the front line?" he asked.

"I don't see anything to the east," said Miller.

"What about the west, near General Sherman's quarters?" asked Quaid.

"There is no fighting," said Miller. "It seems the Union has retreated into the forest."

"Very well," said Quaid. "You can come down now Miller."

Miller shimmied his way to the bottom. Quaid handed him a blue coat once his feet hit the ground. Quaid put on Miller's old grey jacket.

"What are you doing?" asked Miller.

"I need to know where the Rebels are and what they are planning," replied Quaid. "I am going to go behind their lines."

"Dangerous play," said Richard coming up from behind.

"There is more to this than a simple skirmish," said Quaid. "And my company is without artillery."

"Maybe they ain't got many men," said Darren.

"I doubt that," replied Quaid. "Can you get me closer?"

"Sure," said Richard. "Our camp is not far ahead. I think we can cover you in the confusion."

"Great," said Quaid. "Take me as far as you can."

Richard and Darren jumped into the front of the wagon. Quaid and Miller rolled into the back. Richard drove the team hard down the Hamburg road to camp. As they hit the edge of the bivouac, he slowed. Quaid spun off and disappeared into the woods.

He moved with stealth through the brush and tall trees. He moved with surprising speed. Yard after yard Quaid coursed over the terrain. He blended with the leaves. Upon hearing a march he abruptly stopped. He spotted thousands of Confederates. It looked like two brigades. Columns of men lined as far as he could see. They were near Lick Creek. Coming forward was a large contingent of artillery. Quaid squirted down into a ditch on his abdomen. He covered himself with dirt and twigs. He kept quiet as the mass moved past his position. Quaid was anxious. His fifty-fifth Illinois had no cavalry and no artillery. This would be a rout. He needed to get to his company fast. Quaid slithered out from behind the enemy. The Confederates prepared to charge. He increased his speed. Quaid hit the clearing of the peach orchard as a loud Rebel yell arose.

The artillery broke out. The Rebels poured from the woods. The resulting fire was deafening. Bullets and balls buzzed past him like bees. Quaid saw the seventy-first Ohio turn and run. Quaid crossed headlong into the death blossom. He killed as he went. Men were cut down as with an unseen sickle. The artillery pounded the Union's position. Detonated fireballs created so much smoke and dust it burned the eyes. Quaid kept going. He slashed and shot

Confederates at close range. Minie balls whizzed through the brush. The Rebels ran forward. Some were blown backwards as lead burst into their chest. The shot and shell felt like a hundred volcanoes inside a thousand hailstorms. Leaves were stained red. Pieces of stems and fragments of branches flew into the faces of those who charged. Misgivings and doubt spread over the Union line. Panic and pandemonium scattered the boys in blue. Quaid reached his unit. He removed his coat and yelled.

"Fall back!" he screamed.

He waved the men on to a ravine in the woods to the north. The bullets popped and the men fell as they ran. The Rebels came right up to their position.

"They fly! They fly!" shouted the Confederates.

The level of horror rose as the Union boys fled. Quaid continued to kill as he could. He joined his company in the trench. Despite the newly found cover, the fighting became more fierce. Metal pellets were hurled in all directions. Even in the slanted surface of the ravine, slivers of canopy burst and became embedded in their skin. Hollow hits of musket balls tore off arms. Canister shot legs out. Sinew and bone became exposed. With every second, new screams started. And they never stopped. Bodies lay upon bodies. Men no longer resembled men. Pools of blood overflowed and stained the survivors. The mass of humanity became a mass of squirming partials and parts.

For hours the brutality volleyed back-and-forth. Ammunition dried up as the living stole from the dead to perpetuate the slaughter. Quaid crawled from the bushmeat. He felt the need to find his friend. His heart overtook his head. He went looking for Mikey. Twenty yards to the east, Quaid saw a tuft of curly yellow hair pressed against a blue uniform. Quaid ran over the piles of unmoving flesh. He turned the body over. It was Mikey. He was still breathing.

"Thank God," whispered Quaid.

Mikey was in shock. He stared at Quaid as if in a dream. Rattled by the battle, he visibly shook as Quaid sat him up.

"Mikey, it is Matthan," he said. "My cap box is empty. We must go. Grab your hat and get up."

Mikey just sat in stunned silence. After a time he spoke.

"Matthan?" he asked.

"Yes, my friend," replied Quaid.

He helped the boy to his feet. He dusted him off and adjusted his uniform. He handed him his weapon.

"We must move across current," said Quaid. "Follow me through the trench. Once we have cleared the fighting, we will turn north to the landing."

"Why go west?" asked Mikey.

"The Rebels are advancing into parts of the ravine. They are killing at close range. Flanking will keep us from being overrun."

Quaid took off traveling down the trough. He avoided the enemy. Mikey followed closely behind. They stepped on and over the dead. Mikey slowed as he viewed the bullet-ridden corpses. The screams echoed in his ears. The survivors cried in pain, unable to find relief. The wails from the wounded disrupted Mikey's concentration. He tripped over his own feet as the boys begged for help, for God, and for death.

The shelling persisted. The bombing came in bunches of exploding earth and paralyzing claps of thunder. Cannon blasts pulsated. Repetitive shockwaves hurt every sense. Mikey held his hands over the sides of his head. He was frozen in an everlasting storm. He was petrified.

Quaid stopped and went back for him. Mikey was trembling. Just before Quaid got there, a force blew him into the air and onto the ground. Mikey lay with a hole in his chest. His eyes were wide and fixed. Quaid put him against a tree. Metal had broken through Mikey's rib cage. Looking down, Quaid saw his beating heart. Blood flowed from his breast. Mikey tried to talk but no sound came out. Quaid kneeled next to him.

"Be still," said Quaid. "I am here."

Quaid grasped his hand tightly. Mikey stared directly at his friend. His eyes glazed. His heart stopped. His head fell. Quaid could not look. Turning away, he saw a small patch of purple violets. Quaid plucked a flower and placed it in the brim of Mikey's hat.

"Be in peace now, my friend," Quaid whispered. "Peace."

A great groundswell jacked up the hollow of the ravine into a wave bomb. Quaid got up and raced over the falls into the soup. He curled himself into the pit and across the dead. Men in grey suits blew through the backwash in heavy pursuit. Quaid became locked in the blowout. Inside the impact zone, he returned fire. Overgunned, he popped up, cut back and kicked out. Quaid bailed. Once out of range, he rested.

He made his way north. Young soldiers lay motionless in the dirt. These boys would never grow old. They would never marry. They would never have children. They would never be hugged by their mothers. And they would never see another sunrise. Quaid recognized a face. It was Richard. He was on his side. One leg had been ripped off by shrapnel. The bone protruded from the flesh. Its end was cracked and broken. He was pale and still. Not far from Richard, Quaid found Miller. He was face down. He was shot in the back. Quaid turned him over. A cavernous exit wound came out of his chest and an imprint of his body was left pressed into the ground. Quaid bowed his head in sadness.

"Matthan!" shouted a voice from behind.

He turned to see Darren. He was propped against another soldier. He was shot. Quaid raced to his side.

"Darren!" he exclaimed.

"Help me! Help me Matthan!" Darren yelled.

"I am going to get you out of here," said Quaid. "Hang on," he said, as he hoisted him over his shoulder.

Darren howled as he was lifted. Quaid ran like a man being chased by a bear. He moved through the trees, creating distance between them and the Confederate artillery. Quaid continued until he reached a depression in the ground. There he sat Darren down.

He pulled back the darkly stained uniform. His abdomen was split open. Burnt edges of loose skin encircled the hole.

"Can you see him?" asked Darren.

Quaid glanced around. There was nothing.

"Can you see him?" he asked again.

"See who?" asked Quaid.

"That bird," replied Darren. "That little bird."

Quaid peered deep into the boy's eyes. His pupils were large. Darren started to mutter. It was a rhythmic utterance.

"Sweet little bird, sweet, sweet, sweet.
Sing me a song, tweet, tweet, tweet.
Fly me away, fly, fly, fly.
Up to the heavens, high, high, high."

"Darren!" shouted Quaid. "Can you hear me?"

"I'm flying," he said as his life drifted away.

Quaid heard the sounds of war approaching. His sorrow turned to rage. He stepped behind a tree and loaded his guns. A brigade passed by in double time. He came out and fired. He circled in and out of the trees cutting down Confederate skirmishers with a series of close contact kills. Then, he moved on.

The Confederate cavalry came galloping into the arena. The grey riders drove the horseflesh up to Quaid's position. He hurled his daggers. The knives struck several. They fell dead. Gunplay broke open. A barrage came at Quaid. He gained cover and ducked. The bay colored horses continued their charge. Quaid ran for the brush. To save himself, Quaid shot a horse soldier's mount. The animal fell. The fall shattered the rider's leg and trapped him underneath. It broke their formation. The disruption gave him time to escape.

Quaid emerged from the brush sullied and sore. He was tired and thirsty from the fight. He crossed a grassy field and made his way north. Out of the trees rushed a big black Morgan. On his back was a Confederate general in full regalia. Quaid fired the shots he had left. The Morgan continued to charge. Quaid ran but it was on top of him in a few strides. The general pulled his pistol.

He hit Quaid in the arm. The race slowed as another blast caught him in the thigh. Quaid limped on. The Morgan pursued. Quaid spun to face his attacker. A slug struck him in the chest. Quaid fell backward and hit the ground. The ball stuck in his vest pocket, lodged in the pages of his Bible. Quaid gasped for air. The powerful Morgan reared up to crush him. Quaid rolled and the strike only hit earth. He reached for his rifle and fixed its blade. The Morgan stepped back for another run. Quaid was shot to pieces, so he cried out.

"'Lord God, remember me, I pray thee, and strengthen me.'" he said. (Judges 16:28).

He looked into the Morgan's red eyes as it raised. He saw the devil lift its legs to deliver a death blow. Quaid drove the bayonet into the heart of the beast. It tumbled over. The rider was unharmed. Angered by the fall, the general armed his weapon. He walked over and stood above Quaid.

"You are weak flesh," he said in disgust.

The pistol boomed. The bullet tore through his right shoulder. Blood poured from the wound. Quaid placed his left palm against the pain. Red drops dripped from the branded mark of the cross. He felt his life begin to slip away. He crawled closer to the dying Morgan. He placed his hand on the horse.

"Sorry boy," he whispered. "Now go to God."

Quaid got a hard kick in the gut. It sent him all the way over and onto his stomach. The general was furious. He lifted his gun again and squeezed the trigger. Bang! Bang! Two shots embedded in Quaid's back. With his last breath, Quaid uttered.

"'Let the weak say, I am strong.'" (Joel 3:10).

All went to black.

Quaid awoke in terrible pain. It was overwhelming. He groaned as the discomfort came from every part of his body. It felt like his entire back was on fire. He had a large compression bandage on his shoulder. He tried to gain his bearings. The torment disrupted his concentration. Not to be defeated, he tried to sit up.

"Don't try to move," he heard. Quaid turned his head and saw a field surgeon.

"My name is Dr. Murray," he said. "I am the Medical Director here at Savannah."

"Savannah?" asked Quaid.

"Yes," replied Dr. Murray. "You are at Cherry Mansion in Tennessee. It is the hospital."

Quaid stared at him in disbelief.

"You are lucky to be alive," said Dr. Murray. "Actually, I don't know why you aren't dead."

"Thanks for the encouragement," said Quaid sarcastically.

"Many men are still on the battlefield. Yet somehow, you made it here," said Dr. Murray.

Quaid shook his head to get out the cobwebs.

"Look it's late. Tomorrow I have to go to Pittsburgh Landing to treat more troops. You should rest."

Before Dr. Murray could leave, there was a disturbance from behind. The surgeon turned to see General Sherman and General Grant enter the tent.

"We have come to see the boys," said Grant.

"Yes, of course General," replied Dr. Murray.

"Uncle Billy! General Grant!" shouted Quaid loudly.

The generals directed their attention to him. Quaid was bandaged and bruised. Fresh fluid still stained his sheets. Grant walked over to the chair next to his cot. Hanging from the backrest was his uniform. Blood had turned the cloth purple. Grant slowly lowered himself onto the seat.

"Yes, soldier?" he asked.

"May I pray for you?" asked Quaid.

General Grant glanced over his shoulder at Sherman.

"Certainly," he said.

"'The Lord bless thee, and keep thee. The Lord make his face shine upon thee, and be gracious unto thee. The Lord lift up his countenance upon thee, and give thee peace;'" said Quaid. (Numbers 6:24-26).

"Thank you, my friend," said Grant with a heavy heart. "From now on soldier, call me Sam. And what is your name?"

"My name is Matthan," replied Quaid.

"Don't I know you?" asked Sherman.

"I am in the fifth Division, second Brigade. I am a volunteer with the fifty-fifth Illinois. We were together in St. Louis at Benton Barracks," said Quaid.

"Bully for you, boy," said Sherman.

"Thanks Uncle Billy," said Quaid. "It has been an honor to serve under you, and Sam."

Grant stood and walked away from the bed. He took Dr. Murray by the arm and moved him out of listening distance. Sherman joined them.

"Doctor," said Grant. "How is this man doing?"

"He will not survive the night," replied Dr. Murray.

Grant's eyes widened but no expression crossed his face.

"He has multiple wounds, sir," continued Dr. Murray. "If the loss of blood doesn't kill him, the fever will."

Grant briefly stopped and chatted with the other boys. The injured lined both sides of the tent. Sherman went with him. Outside, Grant spoke to Sherman.

"I want you to advance the rank of that Illinois boy," said Grant. "Make him a colonel."

"Why?" asked Sherman.

"A dying man just prayed for me," replied Grant. "That devotion deserves distinction."

Excitement of seeing the generals faded. Fatigue overcame Quaid. He fell into a deep sleep. Hours into his slumber, he awoke in pain. He lay at the end of the field hospital. It was dark. He heard a combination of grunts and groans coming from down the line. He tried to get comfortable. He could not find a position that relieved his distress. He pushed his head back against his pillow in frustration.

A light appeared just outside of the tent's entrance. Someone approached. The brilliance seemed to blur his vision. Quaid blinked in attempt to focus. The radiance came closer. The whiteness of illumination came right up to his bedside.

"Who are you?" asked Quaid.

"Gabriel," said a voice.

The outline of a man became clear.

"I have brought you healing," he said.

"Who are you again?" Quaid inquired.

"As I said, Gabriel," he replied with a smile.

Quaid looked at the black man. He was not in military dress. His shirt and pants were simple cotton coverings. He took the torch he carried, and placed it in a stand at the bedside.

"I have brought you healing," he repeated.

Quaid watched as the torchbearer sat next to him. Gabriel took Quaid's left hand in his. He turned it over and revealed the branded cross.

"It is an old wound," said Quaid.

Gabriel sandwiched Quaid's hand in between his palms. Quaid felt a jolt. The bolt of energy accelerated and traveled up his arm. It increased in velocity and popped through his joints. He felt a crackle and a snap as it moved. His muscles jerked. His mind was lost with respect to time. During the jounce, Quaid saw a golden glow emanate from his fingers. Gabriel whispered under his breath. Then, he set Quaid's hand down.

"I have a salve for you," said Gabriel. "It's my grandmother's recipe."

"What?" asked Quaid still dazed.

Gabriel opened a large jar of white ointment. He removed Quaid's bandage from his shoulder. Gabriel gently applied the balm. It was soothing. His pain resolved.

"That feels great," said Quaid. "Tell Dr. Murray thank you."

"You can thank my grandmother," said Gabriel smiling.

"Maybe I will just thank God," said Quaid.

"I have been called a godsend," said Gabriel.

"Yes," said Quaid. "You are, thank you."

Gabriel carefully removed each and every bandage. One by one, he applied the cream. Afterward, Gabriel covered the wounds with fresh dressings.

"Sleep now," said Gabriel as he readied to leave.

Quaid could no longer keep his eyes open. He slept.

The next morning Quaid was aroused by a commotion of medical officers coming in and out of the hospital. He shouted at a passing surgeon.

"I need to see Dr. Murray!" he exclaimed.

An assistant surgeon stopped and came by his cot.

"Dr. Murray went by boat to Pittsburgh Landing. What can I do for you?" he asked.

"I want to thank him for the wonderful treatment he gave me last night. I think I can return to the battlefield now," said Quaid.

"Are you running a fever?" asked the assistant as he felt his forehead. "You were shot multiple times. It is likely fatal."

"Why do you doctors keep trying to kill me off?" asked Quaid with a laugh.

The assistant surgeon pulled back the bandage from his shoulder. To his amazement, it was clean and dry. He touched the skin.

"No fever," said the assistant. "Your bleeding has stopped. Your wounds appear to be healing. You are a miracle, soldier."

"That is what I have been trying to tell you," said Quaid with a smile.

"I will tell Dr. Murray of your condition when he returns. Meanwhile, rest. You still have a lot of healing to do," said the assistant.

Three days past. Quaid felt renewed. He walked to the end of the hospital and back. It felt good to stretch his legs again. He gazed at the morning sun shining through the tent. It brightened all that was under the canvas. Then, he heard a familiar voice.

"Colonel, Colonel Quaid!" cried the voice loudly.

Quaid saw Dr. Murray walking towards him.

"What do you mean, Colonel?" asked Quaid.

"By order of General Grant, you have been promoted to the rank of colonel," replied Dr. Murray.

"Then I need to get out of this bed. I need to get to my men," said Quaid.

"No sir," said Dr. Murray. "You can have your silver eagles but your regiment will have to wait. You are doing better, but you are nowhere near ready to ride or command. Let alone fight. That's a doctor's order."

"I am grateful for your care. And also for your steward's. He was very hospitable," said Quaid in jest.

"I sent no steward," said Dr. Murray. "Actually, I am surprised that you are alive."

"That is the third time I have heard that sentiment," said Quaid. "It is getting to be a bit monotonous."

Dr. Murray looked at Quaid with a strange curiosity.

"Look doctor," continued Quaid. "A steward came to me three nights ago. He tended to my injuries. I saw my hand glow."

"Yes," said Dr. Murray. "I also saw the Angel's glow on the battlefield the other night. It seems to be some kind of process in the damaged tissue."

Before Quaid could respond, a ward master interrupted.

"I am sorry doctor, but I can no longer control this horse," he said.

"What horse?" asked Dr. Murray.

"There is a black Morgan trying to get into the tent. Every time I tie him up, he gets free. He is quite a demon," said the ward master.

Quaid stood to look. "Can you take me to him?" he asked.

The ward master led Quaid outside. He saw an orderly holding the reins of the black Morgan. Quaid went up to him and stroked his neck. He saw a large scar across his chest.

"Look who came back," said Quaid.

"Is he yours?" asked the orderly.

"I believe he is," replied Quaid.

"Does he have a name?" asked the orderly.

"Call him Demon," said Quaid.

SEVEN

Colonel Matthan Quaid was medically discharged. No longer with cause or country, he headed home. His journey to Illinois was made easier by riding his new horse, Demon. Quaid's physical wounds had healed but his psyche was still in shock. From Pittsburg Landing he traveled over hills, through valleys, and by many forests. A stream of memories filled his thoughts. Rivers of horrors had disembogued armies onto battlefields. Dead soldiers were washed back to a desolate shore. Tributaries of blood pooled over the landscape, staining the soil. Lifeless forms lay face down in just an inch of crimson clay. Men died. Many lives were lost. The sun-soaked bodies became dried and decayed. The war left little resemblance of persons once known. Quaid carried the scars. He carried the scars that never go away.

Days passed when Quaid approached a familiar green pasture. A smile came across his face as he recognized the rise of land. His heart beat faster. He pulled up to a stop, and dismounted. He took Demon by the reins and walked. Matthan wanted to savor every step. With each tread of his boot, he recalled the past. He remembered working in the fields, picnics with Beatrice, and the sound of his son's voice calling his name. Matthan felt the love guide him. Everything seemed brighter. The grass was more green. The sky was more blue. The air was more fresh. He filled his lungs ever so slowly. The flowers of the field shot up in salutation. The bees hummed. The birds of the air sang songs of joy. All seemed right.

Matthan saw the farmhouse door fly open. "Pappy!" came the cry, as his boy ran to greet him. Matthan sped up. He lifted Jacob high and spun him around. The boy embraced him and did not let go. A second figure came following from the farmhouse. For Matthan, it was like seeing Beatrice for the very first time. He walked towards her carrying Jacob on his shoulders. With one arm, he held her close. Great emotion filled their hearts. It was a quiet reunion of serene smiles and tranquil tears. Matthan placed Jacob on Demon's back. He clasped Beatrice's hand. Together they walked to the barn. Beatrice gave him a playful wink and nod. It was good to be home.

"How shall we celebrate, my love?" she asked.

"A slice of your freshly baked pie sounds like heaven to me," replied Matthan.

"A feast," said Beatrice. "I will prepare a grand meal. It will be our finest cheeses, breads, and berries. I shall cook a full chicken. It will be served with carrots, potatoes, and onions. And to top it all off, a tart cherry pie."

"Sounds wonderfully sweet," said Matthan.

"What do you think, Jacob?" asked his mother.

"I am too excited to eat!" he exclaimed. "But I will surely try."

Beatrice packed a full basket. She gathered up some blankets. Matthan carried the supper outside to a nice soft spot. They sat. They ate. They loved. They thanked God.

Days paced along into nights. Matthan became like a caged cat. Week after week the same pattern played out. Nothing tamed his restlessness. He took to drink. It was only to enhance his sleep, but the insomnia returned. Fatigue and agitation occurred. Then came anger. He started to isolate himself. Matthan spent most days in the barn, alone. He lived only in the shadows. He was unshaven and unkempt. He had little interaction, and he ate even less. The seclusion escalated to where he did not return to the house at all.

Beatrice circled the breakfast table as Jacob sat. She had prepared bacon and eggs with toast. A hot pot of coffee hung over the fire. Excited to eat, Jacob slid his chair forward. He readied himself for the food.

"Jacob, did you say your prayers?" asked Beatrice.

"Yes mother," he replied.

"Can you do me a favor then?" she asked.

"Sure," he said.

"Please go to the barn and ask your father to come and join us," said Beatrice.

"Okay," said Jacob.

The boy popped out of his seat like a jack-in-the-box. He sailed out the door and skipped all the way to the barn. He pushed firmly on the large door. The sunlight streamed onto the floor. It exposed the figure of a man laying on the ground. Jacob felt strangely odd. Apprehension toppled over him like a waterfall. He hesitated. He watched his father's chest rise and fall. Sadness struck him. All the joy was squeezed from his heart. Instinct sent Jacob running directly to his dad. He hugged him tightly. It was a caress only a child can give. Engulfed in love, Matthan stirred.

"What is this?" Matthan asked.

"I am saving you, Pappy," replied Jacob.

"Saving me?" questioned Matthan.

"Yes," he replied. "I am saving you. Please Pappy, do not be sad anymore."

The boy's words hit with power. Never had so little been said, and affected so much. Matthan sat up. He held Jacob close.

"You did save me," whispered Matthan. He pulled back slightly and looked into his son's green eyes. "And I want you to keep on saving me," he said.

"Okay," replied Jacob with an innocent confidence.

"I know you will son," said Matthan. "I know you will"

Sunrises and sunsets rose and fell. Matthan worked the farm. He had a renewed vigor. Jacob was a valuable field hand. He started each day with a child's enthusiasm and ended each day with a child's charm. Matthan fed off the energy. His mood soared. His optimism increased and his faith strengthened. Man and boy bonded. Beatrice was encouraged by the change in her husband. All was right again.

Matthan traveled into town. He sold his goods and wares there. He loaded up the flatbed as usual. Jacob sprang from the house and jumped up to the wagon's bench. He was beyond excited. Matthan climbed aboard. They waved goodbye to Beatrice. With the touch of the reins and a giddy-up, the wheels started rolling. Jacob had a tough time sitting still. He moved like every inch of him itched. Matthan simply smiled. He let his boy be a boy. As they went, Matthan tried to remember a day when he felt the same way.

They arrived in town. Matthan stopped to exchange his freight. He told Jacob to remain seated. He quickly concluded his business. And after, he bought Jacob a small sweet from the general store. The sugar seemed to render him mad. Jacob leapt off the wagon and ran down the street. The road was filled with puddles from the night's rain. He jumped up and down in the mud holes. Seeing his son's elation, Matthan took leave of his propriety and hopped in the water right along side him. Both boys bellowed as the liquid splashed in a fountainous spray of slosh. Jacob ran zigzag from pool to pool repeating the action. Matthan laughed as the wet sludge covered each other's pants. He felt freed.

"Okay son," he said. "We need to go."

Jacob stopped and hung his head. He made his way slowly back to the wagon. Matthan followed as three cowboys came upon them in the street.

"Aren't you Quaid?" asked a cowboy.

"Yes," Matthan replied.

"Why aren't you fighting anymore?" he asked. Matthan grabbed Jacob's hand and moved towards the wagon. "War ain't over!" yelled the cowboy.

Matthan lifted Jacob onto the bench. He did not look back. He proceeded around to the other side and climbed on. Without hesitation, he engaged the horses.

"What did those men want?" asked Jacob.

"They were looking for a fight," replied Matthan.

"I can fight them," said Jacob.

"No," said Matthan. "You will not. The Bible says, 'Be not overcome of evil. But overcome evil with good.'" (Romans 12:21). "So just let it be."

The work needed to run the farm was not easy. Matthan got up with the sun and labored all day. He tended to the cows and chickens. They provided milk, butter, cheese, and eggs. He counted and collected the eggs every morning. Matthan noticed that the egg production was decreasing. It seemed like a number of chickens were missing. That evening he set a trap for the predator. Covered by foliage, he positioned himself in sight of the hen house. At nightfall a lone wolf appeared from the woods. It made its way to the coop in the darkness. Matthan steadied his rifle. A single shot broke. The beast dropped. Matthan stood and walked over to the body. He placed the dead wolf in an old sack and carried the corpse to the edge of the woods. He laid it on the grass. Matthan intended to return in the morning for its burial. He wondered about the wolf. He thought it strange that a pack animal was acting alone.

Morning came. Matthan made his way to the woods. He carried a shovel in his hand. Up ahead he saw movement. He cautiously approached. There, next to the burlap bag, he saw a small pup. Matthan knelt down and picked him up. The tiny male was only a few weeks old. Matthan realized that he had just taken the newborn's mother from him. He wrapped the wolf in his jacket and carried the blue-eyed ball of fluff to the farmhouse. From the yard, Matthan yelled for his son. Jacob came hurriedly out the back door and over to his father.

"Jacob," said Matthan. "I have a gift for you."

Matthan rolled back the corner of his coat and revealed the wolf pup. Jacob grinned from ear to ear.

"Is he mine?" asked the boy.

"Yes," replied Matthan. "However, we must convince your mother."

"I promise I will care for him," said Jacob.

"We will put him in the barn for now," said Matthan. "And you promise to be responsible for feeding, watering, and training him?"

"I do! I do!" exclaimed Jacob.

"About your mother," said Matthan. "We need to get on her good side if you are to keep him." Matthan drifted into thought. Jacob waited patiently. "Ah yes," said Matthan. "We shall name him after your mother's favorite author. We can call him Poe." Jacob beamed as Matthan handed him the wolf. The boy held the pup tight. "How could she say no?" asked Matthan.

"How could she?" questioned Jacob in agreement.

The family readied for church, as it was Sunday. Matthan, Beatrice, and Jacob boarded the wagon wearing their best attire. Jacob sat squeezed between his mother and his father. The boy was happy for the new day. He was not as much so for his restrictive clothing. He rode uncomfortably all the way to town.

Outside the chapel, Matthan brought the wagon to a halt. He helped Beatrice to the ground. Jacob followed down. They made their way up the stairs and into the building. The pipe organ blew out a hymn as the three took an empty pew. The small church filled with parishioners. The service started. Jacob did his best to listen. He wanted to please his mother and father by keeping calm.

After the sermon, Matthan and Beatrice said hello to a few neighbors. Hands were shaken and smiles exchanged. Pleasantries were shared in small groups of guests that formed cliques of chitchat. The whispered prattle seemed more like an academic debate than mindless babble. The family made their way slowly to the wagon. With their backs to the crowd, they heard a loud voice call out.

"Run on home, Quaid!" he shouted. "You're good at runnin' "

A hush fell over the assembly. Matthan turned with intensity. No further heckle came. He got his family onto the wagon. Without a word, he drove away. Beatrice understood the grievous slap the harassment struck across her husband's face.

"They do not know," said Beatrice. "You fought. You were injured." Matthan gave no response. "My Love, you deserve to be with your family," Beatrice continued.

"Maybe," mumbled Matthan.

Dinner was quiet that night. Matthan was more reserved than normal. Beatrice tried to engage him.

"Tell me, do you really care what others think?" she asked.

"No," said Matthan.

"Then why so silent?" asked Beatrice.

"Maybe it is because of what I think," replied Matthan.

"What do you mean by that?" she asked. "Certainly you do not see yourself as anything but brave."

"No," said Matthan. "But it has been almost a year now since I returned. Yet, nothing has changed. Soldiers still fight and die. Men and women are still in bondage. And I sit here in comfort as the suffering continues."

"You served," said Beatrice. "You were wounded. You gave full measure."

"Did I?" asked Matthan. "And can I just look away?" He looked off for a second. "I went to war to stop injustice. 'That which is altogether just shall thou follow, that thou mayest live. And inherit the land which the Lord thy God giveth thee,'" he said. (Deuteronomy 16:20). Matthan looked back at Beatrice. "I have my family. I have my land. Still, the unrighteousness remains." he said.

Beatrice reached out and took Matthan's hand.

"Please think on what is here before you make your decision," she said.

"I will," he said earnestly.

He got up from the table and walked outside in search of solitude. Once he was alone, Matthan knelt and prayed. "'O Lord, how long shall I cry, and thou wilt not hear! Even cry out unto thee of violence, and thou wilt not save!'" he shouted. (Habakkuk 1:2). Overcome by emotion, Matthan's oration broke. He waited for a sign. None came. "Help me God," he continued. "Help your servant. I know what I should do, but I know not what to choose." As soon as the words crossed his lips a sense of understanding spread through him. That was the answer. He immediately went to speak to Jacob. Matthan entered his room. He was playing with his toy horses on the floor.

"Son, may I talk to you?" he asked.

"Yes Pappy," replied Jacob.

The boy picked up his toy and stood. He climbed onto his bed and waited. Matthan sat next to him.

"Jacob, I am going back to the war," said Matthan directly.

"Why?" asked Jacob.

"I have to finish what I started," said Matthan.

"What did you start?" asked Jacob.

"Maybe I should phrase that differently," said Matthan. "You see, I made a promise to God… And myself. The promise was to liberate His people from bondage. I must honor that promise. Understand?"

"But you already went to war," said Jacob.

"I know son. But the people are not free. The war continues. I need to help," said Matthan.

"Why you, Pappy?" Jacob asked.

"'Perceive we the love of God, because He lay down his life for us. And we ought to lay down our lives for the brethren,'" said Matthan. (1John 3:16).

"So you might die?" asked Jacob.

"I promise to return when God's work is done," said Matthan.

Jacob hugged his father still not fully assured.

"Time to sleep," said Matthan. "The sun will come up in the morning."

"Okay Pappy," said Jacob.

"Remember to say your prayers," said Matthan as he gently closed the door behind him.

The sun rose. Jacob bounded out of bed. He raced to the kitchen. There was his mother with a plate of pancakes covered in butter and syrup. Jacob's eyes smiled. He plopped down at the table. He mumbled a quick prayer. He then started to carve up the cakes.

"Where is Pappy?" he asked.

"He left early," replied Beatrice. "I think he went to town."

Jacob stuffed his face with flapjacks. A small amount of maple syrup ran from the corner of his mouth. He washed it all down with some cold milk. Some savory bacon complemented the confection of baked batter. Jacob chewed slowly from top to bottom, and then sideways, like a cow. He took pleasure in the taste. The smell was hypnotic. Beatrice reveled in his delight.

Jacob heard a commotion out back as he finished his morning meal. He looked out the window toward the barn. The door was open. He turned around to his mother.

"Pappy is here!" he shouted.

Jacob ran to the barn. He saw his father brushing a white filly. She was a beautiful foal. Matthan noticed his son staring.

"Jacob, this is Angel," he said. "She is yours."

"Really?" Jacob asked excitedly.

"Yes," replied Matthan. "I will be taking Demon with me tomorrow. You will need a horse to help your mother with the chores. Besides, Poe will need a friend to keep him company."

"This is the best news ever!" exclaimed Jacob.

"Come and greet her properly," said Matthan.

It came to the end of March 1863. General Ulysses S. Grant sat in his headquarters outside of Vicksburg. General William T. Sherman joined him to discuss battle plans. General Grant's aide-de-camp entered.

"General, I'm sorry to interrupt," he said.

"What is it?" asked Grant.

"A Colonel Quaid is here to see you Sir," he responded.

"Who?" inquired Grant.

Quaid ducked his head into the commander's post.

"Hello Sam," he said. Quaid stepped forward and also acknowledged general Sherman. "Uncle Billy," he said.

"Do I know you, Colonel?" asked Grant.

"Yes," said Quaid. "Colonel Matthan Quaid of the fifty-fifth Illinois. I am to be assigned my men, Sir."

"Quaid, you say," questioned Grant.

"The casualty from Cherry Mansion?" asked Sherman.

"Aren't you dead?" asked Grant.

"I get that a lot," replied Quaid.

"Your advancement was a brevet, son" said Sherman. "You are no officer."

Grant stood and walked over to Quaid. He took several puffs from his cigar. Grant turned and walked back.

"I am sorry, Colonel," he said. "I have no regiment to give."

Quaid seemed to sink into his own shoulders. He glanced away for a moment. Then a smile began to expand across his face.

"Sam, let me lead the campaign against Vicksburg," he said.

"What!" screamed Sherman. "This is outrageous Colonel!" Sherman's eyes burned in anger. "And you will address General Grant as Sir, Colonel!"

"It's okay General," said Grant. "I did ask him to call on me as a friend."

Quaid looked directly into Grant's eyes.

"Sam, you have been at this for months," he said. Quaid looked over in Sherman's direction. "How did your boys do in the bayou?" he asked.

Sherman scowled.

"Sorry, Sam, but you had no success in the swamp. You wasted weeks digging a ditch. You failed at a frontal assault."

Just then Sherman gave a tempered growl.

"I have a better option," said Quaid.

"Let me hear it," said Grant.

Quaid moved to the topographical map on the table.

"As a diversion, attack here from the north," he said.

Grant and Sherman leaned over the chart.

"Have General Sherman draw Pemberton's attention. Then, send Admiral Porter's gunboats down the river south of the city. Sam, you march the troops west of the Mississippi through Louisiana and meet up with Porter south of Vicksburg. He can then ferry the men across to the east. You can better approach from there."

"The city was attacked before, and it failed," said Sherman sternly.

"Yes, said Quaid. "It must have made for a Christmas humbug.."

Sherman sneered in Grant's direction.

"This time Sam, the navy will not strike, just sail on by the cannon," continued Quaid. "Hug the coastline, and try not to engage. The battlements will have difficulty hitting their targets from the angle of the high cliffs. Once you can control the east it is over.

"Might work," said Grant.

"It will," said Quaid.

"Maybe under dark," said Sherman.

"There is more," said Quaid. "Vicksburg is a rock fortress on a cliff. So, its fall depends on the support of the citizens within. To beat its defenses, I believe you must break the rock from inside out."

Grant and Sherman glanced at each other.

"In the guise of a Confederate soldier I plan to infiltrate and paralyze the muscle of this stronghold," said Quaid.

"Which is?" asked Grant.

"The morale of the men and women of the city," replied Quaid.

"I like it," said Grant. "Matty, go inform Admiral Porter of our plans. I want you to begin the preparation of the gunboats and the transports."

"Yes Sir," said Quaid.

Quaid saluted and left directly.

"Billy, who is our best cavalry man?" asked Grant.

"Our friend from Illinois, Colonel Ben Grierson," replied Sherman.

"Get me Grierson," said Grant. "I have some thoughts of my own."

General Grant marched the men south through Louisiana west of the Mississippi. Admiral Porter secured six ironclads, three transports, and one wooden gun boat. Porter led the convoy on the USS Benton. Quaid followed right behind on the USS Lafayette. The Lafayette was a 280-foot sidewheel steamer. It had been converted to an ironclad in St. Louis. The Lafayette had a repaired wooden river ram lashed to his starboard side and a coal transport behind.

On the night of April 16, 1863 Quaid climbed aboard the Lafayette wearing a Rebel's uniform. He was immediately met by the ship's captain, Henry Walke.

"Who are you?" asked Walke. "And what do you think you are doing?"

"My name is Colonel Quaid," he said. "My orders come directly from General Grant."

Quaid handed Captain Walke his papers. He opened the note and read. A change came across the captain's face.

"I have never seen orders like this before," said Walke.

"Admiral Porter is well aware of my involvement here," said Quaid.

"Very well," said Walke still unsure.

"Captain," said Quaid. "May I ask where are you from?"

"I am from the east," he replied.

"I have family in the east," said Quaid. "But I hail from Illinois. I was trained in St. Louis under General Sherman."

"St. Louis, you say," said Walke. "Then you will feel right at home on the Lafayette. She was converted to an ironclad there and given commission in Cairo."

"I know both places well," said Quaid. "General Grant speaks highly of your service at Fort Henry and Donaldson, Captain. I feel like you are the commander we need."

"I appreciate the general's support," said Walke.

"Cut the engines and dim the lights," said Quaid. "It is time to go dark."

"Release the moorings!" shouted Walke to his crew.

The USS Benton floated down the Mississippi. The fleet of shadowed ships followed. They appeared as ghosts, like apparitions of soulless specters hovering over the water. They sailed south with stealth. Perceptive Rebel spotters identified the outlines of the Union vessels. The lookouts alerted the Confederates on the opposite shore. Tar barrels on the west bank were ignited. It backlit the boats. Bales of cotton along the east coast were set on fire. The light reflected off the ironclads and the transports became visible. An eruption of one hundred guns came from above. It shook the earth and sent seismic waves over the water. Projectiles hurled through the air. The Benton and the Lafayette hugged the banks. Only twenty-five yards separated the ships from shore. The Lafayette unleashed the nine-inch Dahlgren smoothbore gun. It peppered the cliffs. The one-hundred pound Parrot cannon blew powder, smoke, and shell into the air. The explosive chemical propellants discharged like lightning from the decks. Every gun boat now engaged the enemy. The sky brightened like an exploding star.

The Lafayette lost its bearing. It swung sideways. The river's eddy forced the front of the Lafayette to face east. The pounding of Confederate cannon spewed chunks of wood from the paddlewheel housing. It scattered debris across the ship. The pilot house and the captain's quarters were hit, leaving the state room covered in mulch and chips.

Quaid acted quickly. He pushed railing logs overboard. He then followed them in. Quaid swam all out towards the shore. The wet, cold, water took his breath away. Just out from the river's edge, he saw a grooved rock jutting up from the surface. He took hold of a large log and butt it against the stone. Quaid directed the rail at the Lafayette. It struck the hull. The Lafayette's companion coal barge was full ablaze now. It flamed and sunk. As a result however, the Lafayette was redirected south and out of danger. Quaid pulled himself onto the sand. He lay there for a minute, exhausted.

Admiral Porter's fleet had passed Vicksburg. The following day Grant attempted to cross the Mississippi at Grand Gulf. The Confederate batteries were too strong. He sent his men slightly south and traversed the river at Bruinsburg. Grant marched east. Rebels pushed west from the Mississippi capital of Jackson to confront Grant at the Battle of Raymond. The city of Jackson was the main hub for supplies and railways in the south. General Grant's army overwhelmed the southern infantry. The Union put the city to the torch and turned east. Grant met Confederate General Pemberton's army head on and pushed him back to Vicksburg. Grant sent Sherman's troops down the Graveyard Road towards the town. The fighting was fierce and Sherman's forces ultimately failed. The Union fell back and Grant regrouped. He attempted a multipronged assault of Vicksburg from the north, south, and center. The attack stretched across a three-mile front. The Union was again repelled by the Rebels. So they dug in, and General Grant prepared for a prolonged siege.

Darkness fell over the Union camp under Grant. The blockade of Vicksburg was an endless bombardment. The barrage came from east and west. Gunboats pelted the bluffs while army artillery continued to stack up casualties. The only break from the shelling came at meal time.

General Grant slept in the comfort of his tent as the repetitive explosions kindled the city. The resulting creation was a phasing of color with the dark. A small lantern sat by the side of Grant's cot. The general stirred then opened his eyes.

"Trouble sleeping?" came a question out of the night.

"What?" inquired Grant.

A spectre leaned into the light. It was Quaid.

"Sorry Sam," said Quaid. "I had to speak to you."

As Grant sat up, he saw Quaid wearing fresh Confederate clothing.

"How did you get in here?" asked Grant.

"I slipped past your sleeping sentries," said Quaid.

"Sleeping?" asked an irritated Grant.

"They are now," said Quaid.

"Tell me you didn't kill them," said Grant.

"No Sir," replied Quaid.

"Matty, what is this about?" asked Grant.

"I came to give report, Sir," said Quaid.

Grant stared into Quaid's glowing green eyes. They danced in the light of the lamp. Quaid sat relaxed in a camping chair. Grant noticed his new attire.

"Nice looking greatcoat," he said.

"It is," said Quaid. "Thought you should know it is of a British manufacturer."

"Interesting," replied Grant.

"Yes," said Quaid. "Evidence of successful blockade running."

"We will have to address that," said Grant. "So, how does our current difficulty go?"

"I am making progress," said Quaid. "I expect surrender soon."

"Don't think my army will just sit still," said Grant.

"A surrender will come before the boys can break the lines," said Quaid.

"Very well," said Grant. "Get started."

"I already have," said Quaid. "Either by desertion or death, more and more Confederates disappear every day."

In early July, General Pemperton rode out to meet with Grant. They discussed the acquiescence of the city under the shade of a tree. The seige came to a close. Union forces marched into Vicksburg the next morning. The Confederates were given parole. Papers were issued as the Union men shared their rations with the starving. The Rebels stacked up their guns and evacuated.

General Grant strode up the Vicksburg Courthouse stairs. He saw a southern infantry man sitting to his left. His head was down. His features were covered by an old slouch hat. General Grant's presence remained unnoticed. The general stopped and took a few steps to the side. He reached out to the soldier and handed him a small piece of paper. Without looking up, he took the note. Grant leaned closer and whispered.

"General Pemperton had this slipped under his door," said Grant. "Looks like your handwriting."

General Grant moved on. The frozen figure opened the bent scrap. It read. 'If you can't feed us, surrender us. Many Soldiers.'

The Rebel lifted his head. Underneath the hat was the smiling face of Matthan Quaid.

Chapter EIGHT

Quaid continued his service under Grant and Sherman. The Union forces kept up the pressure on the Confederates in the west. Grant used him wherever he could. Under Sherman, Quaid led the strike against the army of General Johnston in the Jackson Expedition. The assault forced Johnston south, and back across the Pearl River.

General Grant was called back to Tennessee. Sherman followed. Under their leadership, the Rebels were pushed out at Chattanooga. Quaid saw much action. Once Tennessee was secured, their attention was turned towards Mississippi. The Union had taken Vicksburg, Mississippi's king. Now they concentrated on Meridian, Mississippi's queen. Sherman ordered Quaid to multiple points of attack throughout the state. He got the Confederates off balance and on the run. The Rebels retreated into Alabama.

In early March of 1864, General Sherman received a communication from General Grant. Sherman called Quaid to his quarters and read the letter out loud.

General Sherman,

As of March tenth, I have been bestowed the rank of Lieutenant General by President Lincoln. I remain in Washington. Send me Colonel Quaid immediately for reassignment.

Yours,
Sam

Quaid looked directly into Shermans stern face.

"Colonel Quaid," said Sherman. "Get your gear son. You are going to Washington. Lieutenant General Grant's orders."

"I will leave at once, Sir," said Quaid.

"Oh, and son," said Sherman. "It has been an honor."

"Thank you, Sir," replied Quaid.

"I am no longer your commander, Matty. You can call me Uncle Billy," he said with a crooked smile.

Quaid rode east. He arrived in Washington and checked into the Willard Hotel. There was a note on his bed that instructed him to meet Grant on the second floor of the president's residency the following day. Quaid retired early. He was weary from the long journey. Sleep overtook him. Quaid found himself deep in a forest. He did not recognize the trees or the terrain. He made a path through the woods. He only became more lost. Quaid rested on a rock to gather his thoughts. He rolled up his sleeves and brushed back his hair under his hat. He heard a loud hiss. From the nothingness, a viper sprung towards the bare skin of his arm. Quaid grasped it firmly behind the head before the fangs sunk into his hand. He threw the snake to the ground. It coiled. Quaid quickly stepped on the serpent, and trapped it under the weight of his foot. The adder looped around and swallowed its own tail. In a gulp, the snake gobbled itself whole, disappearing underneath him. He awoke, slightly shaken.

Quaid cleaned himself up. He dressed, and made his way to the residence of the president. The day was gloomy. The drizzled rain seemed to hang from the clouds. No sun was seen. The dimmed light created an air of negativity. It gave his soul a bitter feeling of despair. Quaid walked Demon to the north side of the house. Through the fog of desolation, Quaid saw the building of white projecting its strength. Four towering pillars held the monumental triangle above. He saw two floors with four sets of windows on each side. The entrance was underneath. The style and symmetry gave the structure a muscular appearance. It was a household and a fortress, flexing its fortitude from front to back.

Quaid trotted by the iron gates and onto a circular gravel drive. He walked Demon to the front door. Quaid tied him loosely to a column under the pass-through, out of the elements. He made his way inside. It all seemed very grand, yet somehow lived in. Quaid climbed the stairs to the second floor. He saw General Grant standing in the corridor which led to the president's cabinet room. Grant approached him. He greeted him with a firm handshake.

"Sam," said Quaid in acknowledgment.

"Matty," said Grant.

"What is this all about?" questioned Quaid.

"I am commander of all Union troops now," said Grant. "We have accomplished great progress in the west. Yet in the east, we have a stalemate. I plan to win this war, Matty. So, I have developed a new approach. It will bring an end to this conflict. And I need you to be a part of it."

"Certainly," said Quaid. "What can I do?"

"I have created the Point Four," said Grant. "It is made of individual men with unique areas of expertise. These men will do what armies and navies cannot. The Point Four will destroy the enemy and its civilian support. I have assigned each member a code name. Red is a cavalryman. White leads the infantry. Blue will secure our naval superiority. And you, Matty, are Black. You will break foreign ties to the Confederacy. You will sever supply routes, cut rat lines, and close money trails. Like Vicksburg, you will sour the population's stomach for war. And you will disrupt operations anyway you can.

"Yes, Sir," replied Quaid. "But I will only answer to you and the president."

"Agreed," said Grant.

General Grant opened the door to the cabinet room. Inside, Quaid saw a long wooden table and chairs. At the end of the room were two large windows. The curtains hung in silence like a mourner's veil. The fireplace was lit. The flames flickered light on a tall thin figure. It was President Lincoln. He had dark hair. It was thick and curly. His beard was choppy but it covered his gaunt features. His eyes were sunken pits of opaque pools. The wrinkles on his face ran deep as ditches. He had no smile. His face was full of worry. It was the worry for his country.

"Mr. President," said Grant. "This is Colonel Quaid. He is the first of the four I spoke to you about."

"Colonel, the general holds you in great esteem. He told me that you are the best of the best fighting men. He assured me that you will change the direction of this war. You have his highest praise," said Lincoln as he stretched out his hand.

Quaid clasped Lincoln's hand securely in affirmation and greeting.

"That is a strong grip you have Colonel," said Lincoln letting go. "You know I was quite the grappler in my day. I believe back then I could've given you a run for your money."

"No, you could not," responded Quaid tersely.

Lincoln glanced aside at Grant.

"May I speak to you alone?" queried a disgruntled Lincoln.

"Certainly, Mr. President," replied Grant.

Lincoln and Grant retreated to the far end of the room. The president glared down upon the general with a strong pessimism.

"You know this man better than I General," said Lincoln. "However, I am unsure of your decision. He has a darkness in him."

"I know he can be hard, Mr. President," said Grant. "His intentions, however, are pure I assure you."

Lincoln strode over to Quaid. He stood toe to toe, assessing him.

"How are you the man to execute this operation?" asked Lincoln.

"Before I answer Mr. President, please indulge me to ask a question of my own," replied Quaid.

"Go ahead," said Lincoln.

"I believe the men and women of this earth are all God's children," he said. "Of His two children, you and I, whom does He love most?"

Mr. Lincoln paused.

"Well said. Very well said," replied Lincoln.

"Mr. President," continued Quaid. "I seek not the power of God, but only the heart of God."

President Lincoln turned to General Grant.

"It is settled then," said Lincoln as he shifted his attention back to Quaid. "Colonel, you are given priority classification as put forward by General Grant."

"Thank you, Sir," said Quaid. "I will not disappoint."

"I believe you," said Lincoln.

"I do have one request," said Quaid.

"Yes?" inquired Lincoln.

"It is that I take orders only from General Grant and yourself, Sir," said Quaid.

"Agreed," said Lincoln.

Quaid nodded at Grant.

"Mr. President," said Quaid. "It was a privilege, Sir."

"Go with God's grace," responded the president.

Quaid walked away leaving behind the two architects of the Union. He made his way down the hallway. A strange sensation hit him as he went. He felt like a set of eyes were on him. Quaid stopped and spun around. He saw the outline of a man sitting in the dark vestibule. There came no words and no movement. He gave it no further thought and turned away.

Inside the cabinet room, General Grant addressed the president.

"Well, Sir, what do you think?" Grant asked.

"I am reminded of a Bible passage," said Lincoln. "'Behold, I will make thee a new sharp threshing instrument having teeth. Thou shalt thresh the mountains, and beat them small, and shalt make the hills as chaffs.'" (Isaiah 41:15).

Quaid returned to his hotel. After a time, a loud knock came pounding on the door. Quaid was not expecting company. He put the book he was reading on the table. He got up from his chair. He twisted the brass knob. Behind the egress was General Grant.

"Matty, may I come in?" he asked.

"Certainly, Sir," replied Quaid.

"We are past that," said Grant.

"Okay Sam," said Quaid. "What can I do for you?"

Grant stepped inside. Quaid closed the door behind him.

"You are to go to Mobile, Alabama," said Grant.

"Very good," said Quaid.

Grant sat. Quaid followed suit.

"It's the last seaport functioning in the south. They still have blockade runners delivering supplies to support the war. I want it stopped. I have notified Admiral Farragut that you are coming," said Grant.

"What is the plan?" asked Quaid.

"Coordinate with Farragut," said Grant. "See if you can be of assistance."

"And if not?" asked Quaid.

"You have free reign to do what you must. How you must," said Grant. "Just bring it all down."

"I will not fail," said Quaid as he got up.

Grant followed suit.

"I know you won't," said Grant. "One and more thing, Matty. Only Farragut knows who you are and the nature of your orders. So be careful."

"I shall," said Quaid.

General Grant reached out with his hand open. Quaid took it in his.

"Good luck, Black," said Grant.

General Grant exited the room. Black shut the door and glanced over to the open book. It was Henry V, by William Shakespeare. Black closed the volume and readied his soul for the fight.

From Washington, Black took Demon deep into the south. In Confederate dress, Black rode directly into enemy territory. He shied away from cities and railways. Black followed the rivers and streams. The trek went across Virginia, past the Carolinas, through Georgia, and into the corner of Florida. He stopped in Pensacola. He sent Admiral Farragut a communication. Black took on extra food and supplies at the layover. He awaited a message back to confirm their rendezvous at Sand Island lighthouse. The report returned as a go. Black loaded Demon for the journey and headed north. He circled over to the west of Mobile.

Black entered into Alabama. Even in the southern stronghold state, Black was at ease with the ruse he used to avoid capture. He rode wearing Rebel grey. He rode unabated until he reached the Alabama River. Black dismounted. He walked Demon along the waterway to find a place to cross. He came upon an old wharf. The pier was crooked and in decay. Most of the boards appeared intact. Black decided to test the worn landing. He left Demon on the bank. He stepped out slowly, checking the planks beneath. The wood creaked under his weight, but held. He reached the end and looked out and over the water. In the river to the north, he saw trees growing through its surface. Black pondered going south to ensure a clean bottom to swim across. He turned around to find Demon when gravity hit him hard. A thrust knocked his feet from under him. His body slammed against the dock. It stung. His chest was in shock from the decelerating strike. Black gasped to get a breath. A force yanked his legs into the drink. His whole form followed with a splash. The wet chill smacked his senses. In an act of desperation, Black struggled to swim. A multitude of tentacles lashed onto him.

The more Quaid fought the tighter became the grip. It was like it had flytrap skin. The unseen Glashtyn dragged him under. Black's air ran short. In the weightless medium of the water, Black acted. He took the water monster deeper. On the bottom he felt for a branch of a tree. He grabbed it, and with a hard pull planted his feet. Firmly grounded, Black peeled the it from his back. He swam to the top. His lungs heaved as he inhaled. Black saw something emerge onto the bank. With a strong stroke, Black followed. It ran on land like a Blue man of the Minch. He wore the Yankee colors. Black chased him. He withdrew and released a blade. The spike struck the back thigh of his attacker. He fell, prone. Black raced up to him and pulled out the knife. The blue mollusk screamed. Black sought to end his squirming as the assailant rolled over.

"Please Stop!" he shouted.

Black grabbed him with his free hand and prepared a final blow.

"Black!" he screamed. "You are Black!"

Black hesitated.

"What did you say?" asked Black.

"You are Black," he repeated. "I saw you in Washington with General Grant. I am Blue."

"Blue?" questioned Black.

"Yes," he replied. "I'm here on General Grant's orders. He assigned me to Mobile Bay. I'm on your side."

Black let go. He looked Blue over carefully. The man was tall. He was a bit taller than Black, but thin. He was thin as a spindle stock with no thread. The bones showed out from each joint. His skin was pale. His hair was flaxen and fine. He had bright blue eyes like the ocean.

"Can you stand?" asked Black.

"No," replied Blue.

"Let me take a look at that leg," said Black.

Black took his knife and cut the pants free. He saw the red juice roll down Blue's thigh. Black tore the material into a thin strip. He applied a tight tourniquet. Blue gave out a cry as it was tied.

"Are you trying to kill me?" asked Blue exasperated.

"Not any more," said Black with a sly smile.

"Great," said Blue under his breath.

"Let me get you to Demon," said Black.

"What?" inquired Blue.

"Relax," said Black. "Demon is my horse. I will take you somewhere safe so you can be mended."

"Okay, I think," said Blue reluctantly.

"Brace yourself," said Black. "This is going to hurt."

Black leaned over and lifted Blue onto his back in one easy motion. Blue groaned. Black carried the casualty of his own creation like a sack of potatoes. The weight barely bothered Black. He set him gently into the saddle.

"There," said Black. "Now you can ride while I walk."

"What about Mobile Bay?" asked Blue. "What about my orders?"

"I will take you there," said Black.

Blue did his best to be stoic as fire shot from his haunch to his hip. Each step Demon took jostled him enough to keep the leg burning. After an hour of aching, Blue asked to stop. Black lifted him off his pedestal. He sat him ever so easily down against a stone. Black unpacked some food and supplies. He watered and fed Demon. Then he turned his attention to Blue.

"Let me see that wound," said Black. The cut had coagulated. "Good, I will stitch you up," said Black.

"How's that?" asked Blue.

"No need for concern," said Black. "I will break out the old housewife."

"Housewife?" inquired Blue.

"Sewing kit," said Black.

"But sew with what?" asked Blue.

"I will boil some of Demon's hair," replied Black.

"You are joking?" inquired Blue.

"No, I am not," replied Black.

He walked over to Demon and cut some hair from his tail. Black placed it in a small pot of boiling water.

"Just give it a couple of minutes," he said.

"You are really doing this?" asked Blue anxiously.

"Calm yourself," said Black. "After my injuries at Pittsburg Landing, I spent weeks in a Union field hospital. I also served under Confederate physicians at Vicksburg. The southern surgeons cooked horse hair to repair their soldiers. They had no supplies available. So they repurposed bandages and used horse hair after boiling them. The Rebel wounded did much better than our Union brothers by the way."

"Okay," said Blue. "I guess I can give it a try."

Black pulled out a jar of honey.

"Oh good," said Blue. "I am hungry."

"This is to put on the gash," said Black.

"What?" asked Blue in a panic.

"I do not have Bromine. This is the next best thing. It may be better," said Black.

"Might as well since I will have horse running through me," said Blue. "This isn't crazy at all."

"You must learn to trust. Then maybe Demon will share his oats with you too," said Black grinning. "I am curious though, how did you recognize me?"

"That day in Washington, I saw you come out from the president's cabinet room. I sat in the corner waiting to go next. After my meeting, I realized you were one of the Point Four as well," said Blue.

"I see," said Black.

"Now my mission is sunk," said Blue sadly.

"Not at all," said Black. "I was headed to Mobile. We can go together."

"But my injury," said Blue.

"With rest and time, I believe you will be healed," said Black.

"You have more faith than I," said Blue.

"Just place yourself in God's hands," said Black.

"I don't share your sentiment," said Blue. "I did once, but no longer."

"Why is that?" asked Black.

"I was once a professor at Bowdoin college in Brunswick. I taught English and Literature," said Blue. "I had a wife. My wife she… She died in childbirth. It was difficult. I raised my little girl, Elena, on my own. She was all that I had. My daughter was of a gentle nature. She was shy and had a good heart. Elena was always smiling with those sparkling blue eyes of hers. My little love was my whole life."

Blue paused. Black continued to listen.

"I was always a good swimmer," said Blue. "I grew up around the water living on the coast. Elena loved the water too. Our best days were spent at the beach. She was always fascinated by the waves. She was enticed by the cool spray of the surf and its pounding white roar. I taught her to swim. One day at the beach, I watched as she ran to the water's edge. She plunged in and swam out. I became concerned and called for her to come back. A massing of clouds came as a violent storm approached. I could barely see her tiny head bobble above the water. I dove in. The faster I swam the quicker the storm came. The clouds broke and a deluge fell. The tide surged and the ocean swelled. The breakers pushed me back. I struggled. I watched as the whitecaps swallowed my sweet child. I stroked harder and harder. I screamed her name. I expended all my energy. The current grabbed me as I gasped against a wall of salt and sea. The undertow dragged me down towards my grave. With my lungs full of liquid, I gave in and passed out."

Blue paused to gather himself.

"The next morning I had somehow washed up on the shore," said Blue. "But Elena was nowhere to be seen. I raised my voice to God in heaven. And He never answered me. I wept right there on my knees, helpless."

Blue wiped the tears from his face.

"I still imagine her out there, alone and scared," said Blue. "God abandoned Elena. He abandoned me. I lost faith the day I lost my little girl. So no, I don't believe in God."

"I am sorry, Blue," said Black. "But God also knows what it is like to lose a child. He shares your sorrow." Black placed his hand gently on his shoulder. "To contain such pain must be like trying to hold back a waterfall," he said.

"I have no family. I have no love," said Blue tearfully.

"You have gained a friend," said Black. "You are not without family. And you will never be without love."

"Thank you," said Blue.

Black nodded. He fixed the two some food. Afterwards, he repaired Blue's injury. As Black worked, Blue talked.

"You know that I volunteered for the Navy," said Blue. "I hoped that the war would kill me. No such luck, I guess."

"So far," said Black sarcastically.

Blue gave a grin. "Somehow, General Grant found me," he said. "He ordered me to Washington. And here I am."

"Great," said Black. "Stuck with a Jolly Tar for the rest of the war."

At daybreak Black made breakfast, along with a couple of cups of stiff coffee. He placed a handful of beans in his pocket for later. The men ate and drank in silence. Black cleared the camp. He loaded up Demon. Before their embarkment, Black checked Blue's dressing. Lastly, Black bent over to pick up the lanky lump.

"Sorry about the trouble," said Blue.

"No trouble," said Black. "It is a little like lifting a lady," he said with a smile.

Blue glanced at the hands that held him. He noticed Black's left hand was covered by a glove. He said nothing. The men continued their journey across the country. Black walked. Demon followed. It was hot. Summer in the south made for a great deal of humidity. Black stopped often for shade. They stayed ahead of dehydration. He kept Demon well tended and rested.

"You have a great horse here," said Blue.

"Yes," said Black leading Demon back onto the trail. "You know what they say. Live for the horse. Die for the ribbon."

"Who says that?... Nobody says that," said an agitated Blue.

"You are the college professor. You should know this stuff," said Black with a grin from under his hat.

As the day drew long, Black again made camp. He carried Blue to a soft spot of leaves he had prepared. Black collected wood for the fire. After dinner, he sat to relax. Black basked in the cool night air. The warmth of the flames massaged his sore muscles. Black pulled the Bible from his vest pocket to read. But he was interrupted.

"Thanks for helping me today," said Blue.

"It is for the cause," said Black.

Blue looked around as his brain searched for something to say. "Tell me, why do you wear just one glove?" he asked.

"It is a long story," replied Black.

"Maybe just show me then," said Blue.

"You are a curious sort," said Black. "Very well."

Black removed the glove from his hand and held it forward. Blue saw the sign of the cross that was branded into the palm.

"I see," said Blue.

"'Who his own self bore our sins in his own body on the tree, that we, being dead to sins, should live unto righteousness by whose stripes ye were healed,'" said Black. (1Peter 2:24).

"And what does that mean, exactly?" asked Blue.

"Through the death of our Lord we have been forgiven by God. And therefore live in His eternal love," replied Black.

"I don't want his love," said Blue angrily.

"My friend, I understand your anger," said Black. "I cannot say I understand God's ways. But I know in my heart that everything He does is meant for good."

"How is the death of a little girl good?" asked Blue with disdain.

"The question is not what was good about a little girl's death" said Black. "It is to ask what was good about that little girl's life. I trust God to know the good."

"I don't trust God!" shouted Blue with heightened emotion.

"Without trust, what is a man?" asked Black. "He is lost."

"I don't care if I'm lost," said Blue.

"God never promised a perfect life. He only promised a perfect afterlife. The cross gives you your life back," said Black.

"Will God give me my little girl back?" asked Blue.

"God loves Elena. He holds her hand in eternity. And he waits there for you," said Black.

Blue was overcome by grief. Tears filled his eyes.

"Do not give up on God," said Black. "He has not given up on you."

Blue regained his composure. "How do you know?" he asked. "How do I know?"

"Because I am here," said Black.

Black got up. He disappeared into the woods. He returned with arms full of broken branches. Black added them to the fire. Then, he stoked the flames. Despite Black's words, Blue remained unconvinced. Unsure of faith, Blue restarted the conversation.

"What is the proof of your belief?" asked Blue.

"Well professor," said Black as he sat. "It is not simply a belief. It is what makes my life. I look at my life, and I see God. In the loves of my life, I feel God. I read the Bible, and I know God."

"Your life is not the life of others," retorted Blue. "And the Bible is just a book. Who can say what is written in it is true?"

"Let me explain how I know," said Black. "First, you have to agree with a certain assumption."

"What is that?" asked Blue.

"You must agree that men and women always act in their own best interests," said Black.

"Okay what about a merciful man?" asked Blue. "Or one of benevolence and generosity?"

"I say that they too are selfish," said Black. "In fact, the giver always gets something in return. And that is the satisfaction of doing a good deed. The euphoric effect benefits themselves. It is what makes people happy. That is acting in their own self-interest."

"What about the priest or the nun?" questioned Blue.

"They receive eternity in heaven," replied Black. "How is that not in their own self-interest? It is most selfish."

"Alright," said Blue. "I will concede to your supposition."

"Good," said Black. "Now consider the twelve disciples. After Jesus was crucified, they hid to keep from being killed. They responded in their own self-interest, preserving their lives. As expected, correct?"

"Yes," said Blue.

"Just days later, they no longer tried to protect those same lives," said Black. "Why did the disciples go against the social imperative?" Black paused. "It is because they knew the truth. Jesus had risen from the dead and they had seen him. They knew he was the son of God. Their earthly lives were no longer part of their best self-interest. It is undeniable," said Black.

Black held out his open hand again and revealed the cross.

"This sign is for you. To save you." said Black. "As for me, the cross appears upside down. It is a reminder that I am unworthy of him."

"Then what can I possibly do to be blessed? To be loved by God?" asked Blue.

"Simply believe," said Black. Black laid down on his side and pulled his blanket over himself. "That is why we find ourselves here. Is it not?" Black asked. He closed his eyes and slept.

The next morning, Black inspected the leg of his friend.

"I am beginning to feel better," said Blue.

"It looks good," said Black.

He hoisted Blue up and carried him to Demon. This time Black was not so gentle in getting Blue on the horse. Blue moaned.

"Yes, you are improving," said Black with a wicked smile.

The men made off for another day of travel through Alabama. After a long while they stopped for a break.

"What is the plan?" asked Blue.

"We are going to do some reconnaissance in the Gulf," said Black. "Then we are to meet up with Admiral Farragut on the Hartford."

"Sounds like a start," said Blue.

"Glad you agree," said Black. "I have been carrying you for far too long. I expect you to do most of the heavy lifting now."

Through the foliage they went. Blue continued to probe his new friend along the way.

"Were you close to your family growing up?" asked Blue.

"Not really," replied Black.

"Why not?" asked Blue.

"My father and I did not get along," said Black.

"Sorry," said Blue. "What about brothers or sisters?"

"I had a baby brother," replied Black. "But I left home before he could walk."

"Where did you go?" inquired Blue.

"The circus," said Black.

"Why the circus?" asked Blue.

"I needed to get away," said Black.

"So you have no friends or family?" asked Blue.

"The circus became my family," said Black. "The strongman showed me how to build my body. The sharpshooter refined my marksmanship. The stunt riders improved my horsemanship. And my old mentor, Andrew, taught me to fence and handle knives. He was a champion swordsman. And he was a great lover of literature. I learned much."

"Really!" burst Blue. "What is your favorite book?"

"Shakespeare's Julius Caesar, I guess," replied Black.

"So, you know Shakespeare," said Blue excitedly.

"Surprised?" asked Black.

"Yes," said Blue in a strong affirmative.

Black glared back at Blue as he sat on Demon like a conquering king.

"'For mine own part, it was Greek to me,'" said Black. (Julius Caesar Act 1,Scene 2).

"Funny," said Blue with a smile. "Who would have thought that Black had a sense of humor? I always thought you were the meanest flyblown piece of meat in the army."

Black stared at him. "That is because I am," he said sternly.

Blue did not know what to make of him. He kept quiet for miles until curiosity finally got control of Blue's tongue. "Do you have a wife, a child?" he asked.

"Yes, a boy," replied Black.

"What is his name?" asked Blue.

"Jacob," said Black.

"Are you close?" asked Blue.

"The war separated us, but my heart has never left home," replied Black.

"Where is home?" asked Blue.

"Illinois," said Black. "My wife and I have a farm there."

"Why do you fight then?" asked Blue.

"I do it for her. I do it for him. I do it for God," said Black. "I have witnessed too much wrongdoing. And I cannot compromise with evil."

"As You Like It," said Blue.

"What?" questioned Black.

"As You Like It," said Blue. "That is my favorite Shakespeare play."

"Sounds right," said Black. "Everyone wants a happy ending."

NINE

Black and Blue reached the beach. Blue was all but new. His leg had healed and he was ready for active duty. The two gazed out over the sea. A gentle breeze drifted across the sand. Black knelt down and splashed the surf on his face. It felt warm like a freshly baked apple pie. The sharp taste of salt tingled from his lips to his tongue. He looked skyward. All around him was blue. No clouds. No trees. The reflected light stung his eyes. Black raised his arm to shade his face from the sun. He smiled as he stood, then glanced back at Blue.

"So it starts," he said.

Black made his way back to Demon. He pulled out the familiar long grey coat and floppy hat from his pack.

"Where are you going?" asked Blue.

"I need to borrow a boat," said Black. "Stay hidden for now. Demon will look after you until I get back."

Blue turned and looked long at the Orcadian creature. He

saw his blood pulse across his arteries and down the dark sinews throughout the skin. Blue took a step back as Demon's wide maw opened. The stench that came forth drove him further from the Nuckelavee. Black laughed.

"He is harmless," said Black. "Maybe get to know him while I am gone."

Blue stared in disbelief. Black walked away leaving Blue to fend for himself. Hours passed. Blue sat in shaded solitary as the Norse devil horse kept watch. A whisper rustled from the woods. Blue sprang up and followed it to the shore. He saw a small fishing boat grounded in the sediment. Black stood beside the wooden craft.

"You borrowed this?" asked Blue.

"Well, I had to explain it to them first," said Black.

"What?" questioned Blue.

"Not to worry," said Black. "They will not be asking any questions."

Blue was at a loss for words.

"I have made arrangements with a local farmer to house Demon while we are away," continued Black. "When I return we can discuss strategy."

"Very well," replied Blue as he looked over the oared vessel.

He climbed inside and drifted off to sleep. Blue awoke to the rocking of the boat. He opened his eyes and saw Black. His attire had changed. He was dressed like an old angler. He carried a rod, net, and tackle.

"Going fishing?" asked Blue.

"It is our cover," said Black. "We need to keep the eyes of Fort Powell off of us."

"Where is my gear?" inquired Blue.

"I need you to swim into the minefield and disarm the torpedoes," said Black.

"You're kidding," said Blue.

"No," said Black. "You are the superior swimmer. And this is your area of expertise."

"So you will sit and enjoy yourself while I risk death?" asked Blue.

"Sounds about right," replied Black with a smile.

"Some strategy session," said Blue under his breath.

The two pushed the boat into the surf. Black climbed in and immediately started rowing. Blue jumped into the stern to avoid being left behind. Black paddled with a strong rhythm towards Fort Powell. Blue sat and sulked. Upon reaching their target, Blue shed his shoes, socks, and shirt. With his dander still up, he dove from the boat. Black watched as Blue's shadow skimmed under the surface and away from view. It was majestic to behold. It was like a seascape painting of a whale done in oils. Black pulled out his pole. He cast the line and waited. The gentle waves of the water swayed the cradled craft. Black closed his eyes as the day grew late.

Black jerked in surprise as Blue seized the ship's side from the depths. He helped his fatigued friend into the boat. Blue lay prostrate and still. He was exhausted from the afternoon of dive work.

"How did it go?" asked Black.

"As expected," replied Blue a bit out of breath.

"Good," said Black.

"And you?" asked Blue.

"No trouble," said Black. "And I caught a couple of fish. I guess dinner is served."

After eating, Blue lay flat and simply stared at the sky. There was just a sliver of moon. The night stars twinkled in the absence of light. As the fire got low, Black got up and gathered more kindling. Blue remained still. His mind swam into an ocean of sadness in the heavens above. He sailed on the waves of sorrow. Blue's heart was heavy. It pounded less and less. It slowed. Blue saw himself sitting on the sand of his past. He grieved. The gloom from inside surrounded his spirit, and choked out the life. His eyes became fixed. His little girl was out there. But where was she, he wondered.

Black returned with several stumps and twigs. He dropped them into the fire. The flames raged upwards. A yellowed grey gleam shone over Blue's bleak expression.

"What is bothering you Blue?" asked Black.

"How can I change it?" asked Blue with a blank stare.

"You cannot," replied Black in understanding.

"You are sure?" asked Blue.

"Yes, my friend," said Black in sympathy. "God puts us all on a path. It is like a piece of string. You go from one end to the other through life."

"What about free will then?" asked Blue.

"Think of the string as having a light side and a dark side across its length. You still must walk along the strand from end to end. As you move along the thread however, your choices are either loving or unloving, light or dark. Being in the light or dark of your choices does not change what comes along the cord. Life's complexities come as the yarn is drawn up into a ball. Your string touches other strings. Sometimes they touch in a small way and sometimes in a great amount. Some just simply cross. Most never touch at all. All the life strings of friends, family, schoolmates, acquaintances, and even passers-by will contact your string. They touch in a longer or shorter fashion to your string. The ball is all the world's strings rolled together. This is the course which God determined for you. Your free will is the choice you make to walk along the dark or the light side of the string. I choose light. I choose love. I choose God's directive. And when I reach the end, He will be waiting for me."

"I never thought about it that way," said Blue.

"God put me across your path, my friend," said Black. "I hope that you come into the light."

As the day began, Black and Blue prepared the boat. They loaded food and water. Black rowed toward Dauphin Island. The water seemed a bit more choppy. Black dropped an anchor to steady the ship. Blue readied himself again and dove in. He immediately resurfaced not far from the craft.

"The current is strong today," he said.

"Oh Odysseus," said Black in a satirical tone. "Have you angered Poseidon yet again?"

"Will you ever stop mocking me?" asked Blue exasperated.

"Maybe," replied Black. "When it stops being fun."

"Great," said Blue in a dispirited murmur. "Can you at least throw me a line?"

"What about the remaining torpedoes?" asked Black.

"I will get to them but I need your help," replied Blue. "I am going to wrap this rope around me. If the undertow becomes too strong I will signal you by tugging on it twice. Then you will have to pull me out."

"Got it!" shouted Black. "Good luck."

Blue got to work. He disarmed the active mines west of Dauphin Island. Upon completion, he tugged the rope two times. Black pulled his partner into the boat. Blue was more exhausted than before. Black sat him up.

""What now?" asked Blue, out of breath.

"We sail to the lighthouse on Sand Island," said Black. "We are to rendezvous there with Admiral Farragut and the Hartford."

"Well get going swabby," said Blue with glee.

"Yes sir," said Black as he raised the anchor.

Black paddled hard for miles. They continued to be cautious. The two did not desire to get caught in a crosscurrent and get pulled out to sea. Black kept up the pace. He put forth his maximum might. The exertion built beads of sweat on his face. His muscle strained as he competed against the living ocean. Blue sat calmly in repose. He watched as Black overpowered the elements.

"There it is !" shouted Blue.

Black stopped his motion for a moment. He looked over his shoulder. On a small stretch of land he saw a crumbled brick building. The remnants of the lighthouse laid in piles of rubble. It had been destroyed by Confederate forces.

"Doesn't look like much shelter," said Blue.

"We will not be there long," said Black.

On the shore, the men took some nourishment. Black made a large signal fire. Soon, the rolling waves produced a large steamship.

Two small rounded boats rowed their way towards them. Ten men disembarked. They wore dark blue navel dress. Blue went to greet them.

"We are Union men," said Blue.

"Captain Jouette sends his regards," said an officer.

"Jouette?" asked Blue.

"Yes, of the Metacomet," responded the officer.

"We were to meet with Admiral Farragut of the Hartford," said Blue.

"My orders are to approach and identify you," said the officer.

"I am Blue. That is Black," said Blue.

The officer glanced behind Blue and took full notice of Black in the background. He slowly leaned his body in toward Blue.

"Are the tales true?" he asked.

Blue hesitated while he stood clueless.

"You know," said the officer. "About him."

"Yes," replied Blue.

"I brought ten men," continued the officer. "Just in case there was trouble."

"Ten is not enough" said Blue.

The officer was shocked by Blue's response. He turned to address his men.

"Let's go boys," he commanded. "Help these gentlemen load their supplies."

Black and Blue entered the launch. They pushed out to the Metacomet through rough water. On arrival the lead officer climbed up first. Black and Blue followed. On the deck stood an average-sized man wearing command attire. He had a round face. On it was a brush mustache. His hair was thin and slicked back. It was Captain Jouette.

"Permission to come aboard?" asked Blue.

"Granted," replied Jouette.

"I am Blue," he said to Jouette. "And this is Black."

"Good to have you along," said Jouette. "A lot has been said about you."

"All good I hope," said Blue with a little laugh.

Black stayed silent.

"Don't know why you boys are here," said Jouette sternly. "Don't care."

"When can I speak with Admiral Farragut?" Black belted out.

"Tomorrow," replied Jouette. "Now why don't you go below and get settled."

"When do we attack?" asked Black undaunted.

"We are delayed. We are waiting for the Tecumseh to come from Florida," said Jouette.

"Tomorrow will be the fourth," said Black.

"So it appears the fifth it is then," said Jouette.

Black glowered at the good captain. Then, he walked slowly away.

"Is he for real?" Jouette asked.

"Everything you heard is accurate," said Blue. "A more ferocious soldier or a more fine soul you will not find. This I know for certain, Sir."

"Then it is good you boys are on our side" said Jouette with a feeling of reassurance.

Black went below. There he strung a hammock to rest. He had worked tirelessly to get himself and Blue to this point. He knew the hardest labor was yet to come. Black had seen battle before on the Mississippi river but this was a more difficult challenge. He felt like the figurative fish out of water. He had faith, however. He also had confidence in Blue and the Union fleet. Nearly asleep, Black heard someone call.

"Colonel!" shouted a sailor. "Captain wants a few words."

"Very well," replied Black.

He rose from his state of recline. He followed the sailor to the Captain's quarters. Black knocked on the door.

"Come in," said Captain Jouette loudly.

Black opened it and stepped inside.

"Have a seat Colonel," said Jouette.

"Thank you, Captain," said Black.

"I am aware of your record," Jouette started. "I also know that your orders come directly from General Grant. That being said, I am in command here Colonel. I expect you to cooperate with my charge and my crew. Chaos in war is destruction."

"I am chaos in war, Captain," said Black. "That is why I am here."

Captain Jouette scowled.

"I understand the concern, Captain," continued Black. "But I know my place. I will assist in any way I can."

"Good," said Jouette.

The captain was still uncertain. He got up from his chair and came around the corner of his desk.

"Colonel, I am experienced in combat," said Jouette. "I know what it means for me and my men. Do you?" Jouette lifted his shirt slightly revealing a scar on his right side. "I got it at Galveston," he said. "We had taken two launches to attack Confederate ships in dock. This is just one memory I have inked into my skin from that day. It was the compliments of a Rebel knife. The other resides on my right arm."

"I see," said Black. "We both carry the scars of battle." Black stood and unbuttoned his shirt. As he pivoted, Black pulled the garment down below his shoulders. Jouette winced at the site of Black's back. "These are mine from Pittsburg Landing," he said. Black fastened up his clothing.

"Then we do understand each other," said Jouette.

"Yes, Captain," said Black. "I believe we do."

Jouette nodded and offered his hand. Black grasped it tightly and gave a firm shake.

Sunrise saw Black standing on the deck of the Metacomet. He looked out over the vast blue deep. He saw a group of sloops of war come sailing forth from the center of the sun. The Hartford led the way. Black and Blue were ferried across to the flagship. Admiral Farragut stood on the main, surrounded by subordinates.

"Permission to board, Admiral?" asked Blue.

"Granted," replied Farragut. "Good to see you boys."

"Likewise," said Blue.

"The men and I were just discussing the attack plan," said Farragut. "Unfortunately, the ironclad, Tecumseh, will not arrive until tomorrow."

"Admiral," began Black. "I want to report that Blue and I disarmed the torpedoes near the pass between Fort Powell and Dauphin Island as we discussed."

"Good work," said Farragut. "We failed there in February. But after speaking with General Grant, I knew we could count on you. We offloaded General Granger and his troops expecting that Black and Blue would come through. Well done."

At present, a signal man stepped forward.

"Message for you, Admiral," he said.

"Yes, what is it?" asked Farragut.

"General Granger has met the enemy. The attack on the confederate forts has begun," he replied.

"Confound it!" shouted Farragut. "We were to coordinate the strike on the fifth."

"Maybe we can launch now," said Blue.

"No," said Farragut. "I want that ironclad monitor from Florida."

"Tell me your battle plan Admiral," said Black.

"We are to sail up the channel to the west of Fort Morgan. Morgan has forty-six guns but only about eight can reach the fleet. Fort Gaines is too far away for its twenty-six guns to cause any harm," relayed Farragut.

"Describe the situation in the channel," said Black. "Are there any difficulties in navigating?"

"It is used by blockade runners," said Farragut. "At the end of June we spotted a twin stacked steamer moving fast through it. It was the Ivanhoe, a runner from Cuba. My gun boat, Glasgow, ran for the beach as it entered the channel. The Glasgow fired several shots and Ivanhoe ran aground. We shelled the ship to no avail. Maybe it was due to the iron plates that were added in Scotland."

"The English," said Black.

"Yes," replied Farragut. "It was tough and irritating. I had to order out the small boats. They boarded and burned the Ivanhoe down."

"Any confederates captured?" asked Black.

"No Rebels and no English," replied Farragut.

"What about the waters near Fort Gaines?" asked Black.

"There are hundreds of yards of pilings built out from the east of Fort Gaines," said Farragut. "Further east, there is a field of torpedoes."

"Were they disabled?" asked Black.

"No," said Farragut. "We tried but we weren't able."

"So there are armed mines in the water just to the west of the runner's channel?" asked Black.

"We believe most, if not all, are no longer functioning," replied Farragut.

Black glanced over at Blue in dismay.

"Admiral, I hope you are right," said Black. "Otherwise, we are fish in a barrel. And that barrel is filled with gunpowder."

Farragut's face soured.

"That is why I wait for the monitor," said Farragut. "The ironclad can provide cover from Fort Morgan to our east. We shall latch together the gunboats to keep the vessels from drifting west into any mines or pilings."

"So tomorrow we go?" asked Black.

"Yes," replied Farragut. "We engage the sphere on the fifth."

"Fittingly appropriate," said Black. "I can only hope we holy warriors do not find ourselves populating that fifth sphere with white lights."

Black turned away.

"What did he say?" asked Farragut of Blue.

"He referenced a poem by Dante Alighieri," said Blue. "In Paradiso, the fifth sphere of heaven holds the souls of the warriors of faith. They were described as bright shining stars in the form of a cross."

"He is a complicated fellow," said Farragut.

"Yes Admiral," said Blue. "That he is. But one you need in a fight."

Blue followed Black to the side of the ship.

"Black," started Blue. "We have much preparation. So, are you in?"

"I am here for you, Blue," replied Black.

"Good," said Blue. "You know, I have not seen battle. Do you have any insights?"

Black stared directly at him.

"'A thousand shall fall at thy side, and ten thousand at thy right hand. But it shall not come nigh thee,'" said Black. (Psm 91:7).

Blue gave Black a look of confusion.

"I am saying have faith my friend. God is with you," said Black.

It was early on August fifth when the call came. "Up all hammocks!" By five forty-five they were under steam. A west wind blew as the flags flew in a mass of color against the sky. Fourteen vessels were latched together in a line. The Hartford was second in the order behind the Brooklyn. Four monitors pushed forward and parallel to the east. Captain Craven commanded the Tecumseh, the lead of the ironclads. Tecumseh fired first. Fort Morgan's artillery opened up. A barrage of cannon erupted from beneath the Union sails. The smoke sat heavy on deck despite the west winds. Admiral Farragut stood on the batten unable to see the action. He courageously climbed up the rigging for a better view. Quartermaster Knowles passed him a lead line and secured it to the shroud.

The Confederate ironclad, Tennessee, came from behind Fort Morgan and moved west. Captain Craven ordered the ship's pilot, Collins, to follow. The navigator veered port, cutting off the Brooklyn and the line of lashed ships. A metallic click fired a flared blast, causing an underwater upheaval. The pursuing Tecumseh had struck a torpedo. The monitor lurched. The bow sunk down. The ironclad rolled right as the stern rose high above the sea's surface like a giant seesaw. The ship's propeller was exposed and still circulating.

It held for a moment. Men leapt from the turret room into the waves. Like a knife into cake the Tecumseh slid below the face of the water.

The Brooklyn slowed her speed. Then it reversed. Behind her the Hartford was pounded by shot. Splinters blew across the main, striking the seamen. Cannon hit the mast sending shards of projectiles into meat and bone. Blood poured over the planks. The sailors scrambled. The Hartford was stuck in obstructed anarchy, and her crew was in jeopardy.

Farragut waved his arms wildly. He yelled down to Captain Drayton.

"Go ahead! Go ahead!" he shouted.

Black locked in on Drayton's beleaguered face.

"Get moving!" shouted Black. "I will inform Jouette."

Black ran to the port side. He grabbed a loose line and stepped onto the rail. Blue ran up to him in the confusion.

"Tecumseh is sinking!" yelled Black. "We need to get to Jouette now!"

Blue seemed stunned.

"Grab on!" shouted Black. "We will swing over the side to the Metacomet!"

Blue climbed onto Black and held on like a child. The circus show duo swayed over to the gunboat. Black dropped down still at high speed. The men hit with a thud. From the paddle box, Jouette witnessed the flight.

"Four bells!" Black shouted. "Four bells!"

Jouette jumped into action. Black pulled an axe from the housing wall. He raised and thrust the weapon, severing the tie lines. Black grabbed Blue by the vest.

"Come on!" he cried.

Black went forward to the rail. He lowered a launch. Blue took over as Black surveyed his surroundings.

"Ensign!" screamed Black. "What is your name?"

"Henry," he replied. "Henry Nields."

"We need you Mister Nields," said Black.

"Yes Sir," said Henry.

"Get in!" commanded Black.

The three hit the water hard. The impact rocked their vessel. Black gave great torque force to the oars and the craft accelerated across the water. He rowed them close to the whirlpool of men drowning in the Tecumseh's wake. Blue stripped off his shirt and shoes. He dove in headfirst. Blue plucked the sailors from the water one by one. He handed each man to Henry and Black. Blue gathered ten in all.

The Hartford steamed forward fast. It beat back the Confederate gunboat, CSS Gaines. Black watched as the ship tried to limp away.

"Blue get the boys back to the Metacomet," said Black. "I am going after the Gaines."

"What?" questioned Blue.

"You heard me," said Black.

He looked over at the ensign.

"Good work, son," he said. "Keep going."

Black removed his shoes and jumped. He swam straight as a missile at the Gaines. He powered through the waves. His kick and stroke burst out of the water with determination. He came upon the iron plated hull of the Gaines. He was wet and weary. He lost his glove in the swim. Barehanded, he clasped a fallen lead line. Black lifted himself up and slid onto the deck. He took out three seamen and tossed them overboard. He quickly moved to the stern. Black yanked the Gaines' flag pole from its fastenings. He struck an attacking boatswain with it, knocking him unconscious. Black slammed the rod into the spinning paddles of the steamer. The boat jerked as the blades broke off. Black staggered. Rebel sailors rushed past the sidewheel. Black steadied himself. He turned and fired a swivel cannon. The metal ball crashed into the mast. Bits of wood burst into pieces. The force blew the Rebels backwards. The mast crumbled and fell. It crushed the housing, trapping the remaining seamen below.

Out of the ruins, Black heard a loud yell.

"Answer to me Yank!" it screamed.

Black saw a tall man standing next to the housing. He had dark hair and darker eyes. The brows above them were big and bushy. His nose was long and pointed. The high bones of his cheeks pushed up. A thin anchor beard and matching mustache filled in his face. He held a sabre in his hand. Black stared for a minute.

"Dag Engel," said Black in recognition.

"So you know me?" asked Dag. "Very good. Then you know you cannot defeat me, Yankee."

"'Words before blows. Is it so,'" said Black. (Julius Caesar Act 5 Scene 1).

"Impressive, for a brute," said Dag. "Shakespeare from the mouth of a savage."

"Enough talk!" yelled Black.

Black hurled a lightning fast blade his way. Dag raised his sword and knocked the pike out of the sky.

"You Yanks, always in a hurry," said Dag. "No time for proper etiquette. No time for refinement."

"You are not refined," said Black. "You are just another cruel tyrant who has deluded himself into thinking himself a king."

"I am champion!" declared Dag. "If I was not an English gentlemen, I would cut you down without delay."

Dag reached over and took up another sabre. He tossed the sword to Black.

"Lucky for you I am principled," said Dag.

"Your only principle is counting your coins and adding to your ill-gotten reputation," said Black.

Dag fumed. "No more niceties," he shouted. "En garde!"

Black took the sabre in his left hand. He squeezed the hilt of brass wire bound to leather. He felt a surge of strength go from his palm to the grip. The men rushed each other. They clashed as metal struck metal. It was force opposing skill, power versus finesse, and might meeting mastery. Again and again the swordsmen met. Engage and attack. Guard and parry. Lunge and feint. In a moment of hesitation, Dag struck just above Black's guard. He drew blood. The red ran down Black's wrist. The pommel became saturated. His control of the sabre slipped. Dag maneuvered Black up against the side of the housing. He took advantage and sliced the skin right through Black's shirt. The shredded material bled. Black changed hands and moved his sabre from left to right. He thrust it forward. Dag countered, and drove his sword into Black's right shoulder. It came out the other side and pinned him to the wall.

"You are beaten," said Dag smiling.

Black could no longer hold his sabre. It fell. Dag grinned as he pushed the blade in farther. Black grimaced as Dag moved close. In the blink of an eye, Black lifted his left hand and snatched Dag's arm. Black broke the bones. Dag dropped his sword in pain. Black yanked the spike from his shoulder and freed himself. He crushed his wrist again. Dag screamed in agony.

"If it offends," shouted Black. "Cut it off!"

Black slashed his sabre down and Dag howled as his hand hit the ground.

"Andrew says 'Hello'," said Black with a brutish heart.

Black dove off the deck of the burning boat. With no rudder, the Gaines ran adrift. The fires scorched the ship to the waterline. The charred old wood smoldered and sunk. Black swam for the Hartford and home. Aboard the flagship he met up with Farragut, and Blue from the Metacomet. The powerful Confederate ironclad, Tennessee, was captured. It was a Union victory.

"Good to see you again Black," said Blue. "After you left, I wasn't sure I would."

"All is well," said Black. "You and I are both alive, my friend. But there is more fighting yet to come in this war. Shall we continue?"

"No," replied Blue. "I am going to stay with the Metacomet. We are mounting a humanitarian mission to take the injured to Pensacola. Admiral Farragut has ordered us to carry both northern and southern wounded back for care.

"Very well," said Black. "I understand. 'For he who serves Christ in these things is acceptable to God and approved by men,'" said Black. (Romans 14:18).

"Thanks," said Blue.

He smiled at his friend. Black gently placed his arm around Blue's shoulder.

"Demon will miss you, you know," said Black laughing.

"Of that I have no doubt," said Blue in reply.

Chapter TEN

Black backtracked and collected Demon. Reunited, the pair ventured into Georgia. Its male population was depleted from the war. This left villages and plantations vulnerable. Black rode through these southern settlements for the purpose of diminishing civilian support. Black's attacks were a combination of agitation and elimination of the enemy. He set slaves free. He put men, women, and children on an underground path to the north. Black caused the number of fatalities in the Confederate States to increase. He spread fear by burning the bodies in large mounds of threes. Black identified himself to both slaves and survivors by revealing the sign of the cross on his hand. The symbol became synonymous with terror. Citizens were scared. His name drew fame as the Black Death.

The Confederate government moved to stop him. President Jefferson Davis instructed Secretary of State, James Seddon, to put an end to the Black Death. An execution squad of cavalry was chosen. They were the worst of the worst. Each man had a hatred of the Union, and a love of violence. The horse soldiers were ordered to track down the Black Death and assassinate him. The killing corps rode forth with a single directive. Now Black became the hunted.

Black was alone in the night. He gazed out at the moon-soaked fields of cotton. The mirrored twilight sparkled like a reflecting pool. Black beheld nature's beauty. The silent woolgatherer got lost in his own intellect. He drifted. His mind was a ship on the water. He floated. His psyche sailed away from all reason. Black felt the cool sea breeze blow across his face. The gentle wind took him to his wife and son. He saw them sitting on a blanket of flowers. The aroma was fragrant. The sweet air whispered to him. Black followed the puffs to the base of a hill. He saw his family at the top. Slowly, Black climbed. He moved ahead in noctambulation. The hill got higher as he walked. His ascent stalled. The illusion faded and his wife and son dissolved. Black gave a gasp as he found himself standing in the dark, alone again.

Black took an arrow from his quiver and set the tip ablaze. He launched it into the air. The semicircular flight of the flame flew through the darkness. The dart landed in the center of the cotton field. The flash ignited the fibers. The resulting burn lit up the night. Waves of yellow and red flowed over the property. The pasture smoked as the plantation owners ran from the estate. The governors engaged their slaves in combating the fire. Black used his bow to take down the landowners one after another. Proprietor, partners, headman, and foreman dropped as unseen arrows found their mark. The slaves remained fixed and afraid as death shot all around them.

A nonchalant Black strolled up the alleyed drive toward the main house. Halfway past the line of oak trees, shouts and screams echoed in a mix of gunfire. Black heard the pops. He turned. Four horsemen appeared out of nowhere. They rode fast. The horsemen spit bullets like a pestilence. Everyone broke and ran. The warlords cut down the workers with the sword as they scrambled. The horsemen drove back and forth until they trampled the slaves against the cinders of the crops. The smell of their burnt bodies spread over the air. The mounted men galloped at Black in anger. Black scurried directly into the line of oaks as a spray of lead balls blew holes into the trunks. He quickly made his way for a tiny log cabin. He lowered his shoulder and crashed into the planks of wood that served as a door. His body smashed onto the floor. Bullets rebounded around the room and blasts burst off its exterior. He saw a woman and her daughter standing in the middle of the nightmare. Black raised up and turned over a table. More projectiles riddled the interior. He ducked. Lifting his head, Black saw the woman and child laying in the corner, dead. He then heard a strange sound. He saw a small boy staring at his mother and sister. Black grabbed him and pulled the boy behind the butcher's block. Chips of timber filled the space again as Black held the boy close.

"Do not look," said Black. "You cannot help them now."

The young slave shuddered in Black's arms.

"I am sorry," said Black. "But we must run when they reload."

The boy was traumatized.

"I am Matty," said Black. "What is your name?"

"Squash," said the boy sheepishly.

"Good man," said Black. "You must do as I say. Okay?"

"Yes sir," replied Squash.

"Call me Matty," said Black.

"Okay," said Squash.

"Excellent," said Black. "Now little brother, I need you to grab onto my neck like you are riding a horse."

"But I don't know how to ride," responded Squash.

The shooting stopped.

"Come little brother," said Black. "Time to go."

Black pulled his six-shooter and stood. With his left hand he lifted Squash by the seat of his pants and carried him through the door. He ran with his gun blazing. A volleyed response came as Black ran for the cover of the woods. At the edge of the wilderness, he was clipped by a slug in the side of his thigh. Black fell forward and Squash toppled over him. The two tumbled into the weeds. Black reached out his hand to the young man.

"Come on little brother," said Black. "We are almost there."

Squash clutched on. They lumbered away, each leaning on the other. Black pushed through the brush the best he could on a wounded leg. His thigh burned like the sun. The searing pain did not hide the feeling of fluid flowing down his pants, however. They became damp. Black spotted a rock where the runaways could catch their breath. They rested. Black leaned his back against the stone. Squash crouched next to him. He looked over at the boy and smiled.

"Are you hurt?" asked Black.

"No," replied Squash.

"Good," said Black.

He removed his belt from his waist. He wrapped it around his leg and pulled the tourniquet tight.

"We will need to keep moving," said Black.

"Yes sir," said Squash.

Black gently placed his hand on the boy's shoulder. He was shaking.

"Squash," said Black. "I need you to help me."

"Yes sir," said Squash.

"Squash," said Black. "We are brothers now. Call me Matty."

"Okay," said the boy.

"Help me to my feet," said Black.

"Yes brother," said Squash.

Black put all his weight onto his left leg. He pushed himself up, erect. He wobbled a bit as his right foot touched the ground. Squash brought him back to vertical.

"How can you run like this?" asked Squash.

"I cannot," said Black.

Black gave a loud whistle. Squash heard the bushes rustle. The hair on the back of his neck tingled. He felt cold. Squash saw a large beast approach. He squeezed Black's arm and shut his eyes.

"Do not be afraid," said Black. "He is a friend."

Squash took a look. He saw a great horse. It was Demon.

"He is our ride," said Black.

Black gave Demon a pat on the neck and a rub on the nose. He cautiously hoisted himself into the saddle. Black swayed slightly to one side. With one arm he picked up Squash and placed him behind his back.

"Hang on," said Black.

"I will," replied Squash nervously.

Squash held fast as Demon started off slowly. Black's discomfort increased with every stride. His thigh throbbed with the motion. He grit his teeth and swallowed his suffering. The pain continued to build. Black pulled back on the reins and Demon came to a halt.

"Squash," said Black. "We must circle back."

"What?" questioned Squash.

"I cannot ride much further," said Black. "And I cannot run."

"Please, no," said Squash.

"Those men will catch us. We have to go back," said Black. "It is our best chance. They will not look for us there. In a few days time, we can make our way to freedom."

Squash was silent.

"Be brave little brother. We will protect each other," said Black.

Squash smiled at him. Black turned Demon around and headed for the plantation. He drove him to the front of the main house. Black lowered Squash down then descended himself. He secured Demon to a tree. Squash helped Black climb the stairs to the porch.

"What now?" he asked.

"We will knock," said Black. "And we must not forget our manners."

Black beat on the door. As he heard the handle unlatch, Black moved the boy behind him. A middle-aged woman opened it. She wore a dark brown colored dress. It came in at the waist and spread at the bottom. Solid buttons ran in single file from her neck to her midriff. Wavy white lace enriched her collar and cuffs. She stared at Black's long grey coat. The unfastened cloak displayed the dried blood on his injured leg.

"Madam..." started Black.

"Come in sir," she said anxiously.

She stepped back and Black strode inside. Squash followed and came around to the front. The woman gasped.

"What is this?" she asked.

"This, as you may know, is Squash, Madam," said Black. "May I inquire as to your name?"

"I am Mary Louise Mosbey," she replied. "Who are you? And what is this about?"

Black removed the glove from his left hand. He held it out for her to see.

"I believe you know who I am, Madam," said Black.

Mary Louise shook. The blood drained from her face.

"We seek shelter," Black continued.

"And if I refuse?" Mary Louise asked.

"Do you think a refusal would be wise?" asked Black.

"Come in then," said Mary Louise reluctantly.

"Thank you, Madam," said Black. He removed his hat and turned toward Squash. "Little Brother the mistress has offered us her care," said Black.

"Thank you, Miss," said Squash.

"We are thankful, Madam. Let us keep it that way," said Black.

Black moved into the parlor. He sat and rested his leg on the couch. He took a blade and cut his pants free. The injury was fresh but the blood had congealed.

"Madam," said Black. "May I trouble you for some water and clean strips of cloth?" He made Mary Louise's skin crawl. She smoldered inside. "Squash can help you," he said.

"No need," Mary Louise replied as she walked out in a huff.

Black motioned to Squash. "Go sit by the fire," he said. "Get warm."

Squash got comfortable by the flames. Mary Louise returned

with a pitcher of water and a washing bowl. She pulled several strips of white cotton cloth from her pocket and laid them on the table.

"Thank you, Madam," said Black. Mary Louise gave Black a long look of contempt. "We will be fine right here for the night," said Black. "You may go." A mortified Mary Louise stormed out of the room. As she left, Black called out to her. "But do not go too far," he yelled.

Black chuckled. He looked over at Squash crouched by the fire. "Come here for a second little brother," he said.

Squash got up and stepped towards him.

"Are you thirsty?" Black asked.

Squash nodded yes. Black lifted the pitcher over the bowl. "Cup your hands," he said. Squash curved his fingers and put his palms together. Black filled his hands with water. "Drink," said Black.

Squash brought his hands to his mouth. He sipped and swallowed the liquid. A bit dripped down into the bowl. Black poured in the extra from the pitcher. He soaked the cotton strips in the water. After squeezing out the excess, he cleaned the rent on his leg. He wiped away the dried blood and debris. Black bent his knee so he could apply a dressing. He winced for a second when he tugged to tie it.

"It has been a long day," said Black. "Go and rest by the fire, Squash."

Squash did not move.

"Do not worry, little brother," said Black. "I will be well again soon. Now, sleep."

In the morning, Black awoke to pain and stiffness. He glanced around the room. Squash was still sleeping. He slowly lifted his feet and placed them on the floor. Black stood. Before moving forward, he steadied himself on the davenport. He walked gingerly to the kitchen. He looked around for food. Black saw some fruit sitting on the table. He continued his search at the large open fire in the corner of the cookhouse. He grabbed a pot to make coffee. It was empty. A soft sigh came from behind him, like a kitten stretching. He turned to see Squash standing there.

"Squash," said Black. "Could you please fill this pot with water from the well?"

"Sure," replied Squash.

"Thank you," said Black.

He handed the boy the large black kettle. Squash made his way outside. Meanwhile, Black scoured the kitchen. He found cornmeal in a cupboard and some salt pork. Black chopped the pork into thin strips and placed them in an iron pan. He placed it on the fire. He immediately caught the aroma of the grease popping in the pan. The smell of charred meat rose with a life of its own and traveled throughout the house. Black was taken by the hypnotic smell. His trance ended with two loudly spoken words.

"Good morning!" said Mary Louise. "My vagrants are still here I see."

"It is because you are such a gracious host," said Black sarcastically.

"And you make my blood boil, sir," said Mary Louise.

"Good," said Black.

"Is that a threat?" asked Mary Louise.

"Why no, Madam," replied Black. "I am a civilized man."

Mary Louise stormed away. Before she was out of earshot, Black yelled. "I could do with a new pair of trousers, if you please," he cried.

Squash entered the kitchen. Black took the coffee beans from his pocket and placed them on the counter. He crushed them with a small mallet and added the mash to the kettle. Soon the coffee was boiling. It added a nutty scent to the air. Black removed the cooked bacon from the fire. He placed the pork on a plate and poured the leftover grease into the cornmeal. He rolled the mixture until it formed a firm yellow ball. Black divided the dough into long strands. He put the pencil-appearing pastes on the fire.

"We call this sloosh," said Black. "Shall we sit?"

Black set out three plates. He filled each with food. The two sat at the table.

"Shall I say grace?" asked Black.

"What is that?" asked Squash.

"It is better if I show you," replied Black. "Dear Father, God of heaven and earth, please bless this food to the nourishment of our bodies. Amen"

The boys finished their meal in silence. Afterwards, Black cleaned the dishes. He stacked the cups and plates on the counter. He left the one untouched portion on the table.

"Squash," Black started. "I need to feed and water Demon. I could use a hand."

"Happy to help you brother," said Squash.

"Good," said Black. "We will take Demon to the barn. Then we will get him settled."

Squash got up and headed for the front door. Black followed. He limped along slowly. In the anteroom, Black saw a rounded cylinder. It held three walking canes. They were made of wood. Two appeared brown in color. The third was wrapped in black leather. Its bulbous end contained a carved serpent's head. Black took it up. He put pressure on the crutch and moved to catch up with Squash.

Demon was let loose. The unrestrained animal trotted around. Black made for the barn. Upon arrival, he gave a loud whistle. Demon immediately came running. Black directed Squash in his feeding. Once Demon was settled, Black and Squash cared for the plantation's other animals. It was a full day's work. The labor was strenuous but at least it kept them away from the house and Mary Louise.

"That is enough for today," said Black. "Besides, I think we deserve a drink."

"Yes brother," said Squash enthusiastically.

"I am curious, where did you get the name, Squash?" asked Black.

"Some of the older kids thought that my head was shaped like a squash," he said sadly.

"Sorry little brother, I did not mean to be hurtful," said Black. "I think Squash is a unique name, a special name. And I like it. I like it a lot."

Squash smiled.

"You think so?" he asked.

"There is nobody like you, little brother, in all of God's green earth. That is something to be celebrated," said Black.

A sweaty Black and a tired Squash entered the main house. They were met at the door by Mary Louise. Black paused and rested his weight on the thin stick at his side.

"I want to thank you for doing the chores today," said Mary Louise.

"You are most welcome," said Black. "We plan to earn our keep, Madam."

"May I offer you some water?" she asked.

"It would be much appreciated, Madam," said Black.

Mary Louise headed for the kitchen. The boys went back to their resting places in the parlor. Mary Louise returned with two cups full to the brim. The thirsty workers gulped down the contents. Mary Louise gathered the glasses and whisked them away.

"Thank you, Madam," said Black as she left the room.

Black sat back and allowed his muscles to relax. He took out the small Bible from his chest pocket. He wanted to read before he lost the light of day.

"What is that book?" asked Squash.

"It is the Bible," replied Black.

"The Bible?" inquired Squash.

"Yes," said Black. "It is the word of God."

Squash's small face showed ignorance.

"God is our creator," said Black. "He made us. He made the world and all that we know to be good."

"Where is He now?" asked Squash.

"He is here," replied Black. "God is everywhere. He is in the sun, the wind, the trees, the land, and the seas."

"Can I see Him?" asked Squash.

"Yes," replied Black. "Just look around."

"I don't understand," said Squash.

"God is all things. He is in all things," said Black.

"But if I can't see Him, how do I know He is here?" asked Squash.

"By His love. Above all, God is love," said Black.

Black held up the Bible. "In here we can find it. It says this. 'God is love. And he that dwelleth in love dwelleth in God. And God in him,'" said Black. (1John 4:16).

"Can you tell me more?" asked Squash.

"I will read it to you," said Black. "'Herein is our love made perfect that we may have boldness in the day of judgment. Because as He is, so are we in this world. There is no fear in love but perfect love casteth out fear. Because fear hath torment. He that fearth is not made perfect in love. We love Him, because He first loved us. If a man say, I love God, and hateth his brother, he is a liar. For he that loveth not his brother whom he hath seen, how can he love God whom he hath not seen? And this commandment have we from him. That he who loveth God love his brother also.'" (1 John 4:17-21).

"Then I also love God," said Squash. "Because I love my big brother."

Black felt a warmth he had not known since before the war. The feeling evaporated when Mary Louise saw him reading to the boy.

"What are you doing?" she shouted. "You are forbidden to teach him!"

"He needs to know about God," said Black sternly. "All must know about God."

"Not in my house," said Mary Louise.

"This is God's house," said Black. "Everything belongs to God."

"I will not be lectured in my own home, nor will I stand for this outrage," said Mary Louise.

Just then, Squash darted over to her. He put his arms around her waist and squeezed. "Miss," said Squash. "Please do not be upset so."

Mary Louise was shaken by the act of kindness. Words failed her. She remained motionless and was at a loss for where to place her hands.

"God is telling you He is here, Madam," said Black. "He always has been and always will be."

Mary Louise pulled away from the embrace. She quickly left the room without speaking.

The next few days the parties kept their distance. Black grew stronger with every sunrise. The pain subsided. His step became uniform and steady. He was his old self again. As Black gathered fresh water from the well one morning, his thoughts turned to God's grace. His heart was reassured by the healing power of God's love. He re-entered the house revived and re-energized. He was as new.

An incendiary disturbance ripped into the front hall. Black raced to the detonation. As he rounded the corner, he spotted four men with guns drawn. Slivers of wood were scattered on the floor from the broken door. He saw a petrified Squash standing on the stairs.

"Run!" yelled Black.

Squash dashed up the steps. Bang! A shot rang out. Squash fell forward with red running from the hole in his back.

"No!" screamed Black.

He grabbed the wrist of the gunmen nearest him and broke his arm. The three others turned. Black drew his knife and slashed an intruder low across the leg. Bullets blast past his head. He rose up and drove the long blade into the next's chest. Powder filled the air like a mushroom cloud. A fireball grazed his shoulder but it did not impede his progress. He struck the last assassin with a forceful blow. Black picked up the shooter and flung him through the glass window. He retrieved a strayed revolver from the floor and put a slug into each thug, ending the brawl. He saw Squash laying on the landing. He ran up the stairs to his lifeless form. Black rolled Squash over and took him in his arms.

"Little brother," said Black. "I am here."

"I am sorry brother," said Squash softly. "I tried to..."

His beating heart stopped. The last ounce of oxygen escaped from his lungs. Black's eyes filled. He held him affectionately.

"No little brother," he whispered. "Not you."

Time stood still. Black sat there for what seemed like hours. All the gifts God had given him and he could not save this one child. His spirit was crushed. Black carried the boy outside. He gently placed him under the shade of a tree. His genteel head slipped to one side as Black set him down. His anguish turned to anger. He plunged into fury and marched back inside. Black dragged the killer's bodies to the pig pen and with contempt he dumped them in.

"Let them sink into the pit that they made," he hissed.

Black returned to find his friend resting in silence. He got down on one knee and prayed. He lifted the boy up, and in tenderness held him against his chest. He walked slowly away from the house.

"Stop!" yelled Mary Louise.

Black rotated around. Mary Louise pointed a pistol at him. Black glared back in spite.

"Anyone can find courage behind the barrel of a gun," said Black. "Real courage comes when you love someone who does not love you back. Like this dead boy did."

"You did this!" she screamed. "My house and my land are ruined. It is all because you came down here!"

"I did not start this," said Black.

"No?" said Mary Louise. "Well, you will go no further."

Black stepped in her direction. Mary Louise became agitated. Black saw her shaking. He kept walking anyway.

"Maybe you held a gun before. Maybe you even pulled the trigger," said Black. "But killing a man is much different you will find."

Mary Louise hesitated. Her eyes shifted from side to side. She pushed the weapon out farther at Black.

"Do not make me lose my manners, Madam," said Black.

Mary Louise dropped the gun. She fell down upon herself and cried. Black gave a sigh in sympathy.

"Madam," said Black. "There are not enough tears in the entirety of humanity to wash away the transgressions of this war. The bloodshed stains us both."

Black carried Squash all the way off of the plantation. He found a towering oak tree. Its limbs reached high into the sky. Its leaves covered the ground like a blanket. Black opened the earth beneath it and placed Squash in. He spread the fresh soil over him and marked the grave with a cross carved into the trunk of the tree. Below, he left only one word. Squash.

Chapter ELEVEN

The strongest man in the Union was broken. His heart was fragmented and the pieces were crushed under the weight of his loss. Black ate little and slept even less. His skin thinned, and later yellowed. He was gaunt. Without hope, Black was hollow. His direction was gone. He no longer had the will to fight. Black wandered aimlessly through the wilderness. He abandoned his ideals while Demon hauled him across the grasslands of despair.

At the end of too many days, exhaustion overcame him. He passed out underneath a small sapling. Black entered a dreamworld of complete darkness. He arose in an inky amorphous space that asphyxiated all sound. A dim crepuscular light grew in front of him like a gathering fog. He made out the contour of an oak tree. He walked cautiously toward it. As he moved closer, he saw a small silhouette. Black advanced at the phantasm. His eyes accommodated. The convergence revealed the back of a child kneeling. As Black neared the vision, he heard vague whisperings.

"'Though I walk through the valley of the shadow of death...'" it said. (Psm 23:4).

The specter suddenly stopped. His head turned. Fiery eyes of red burned without flames. Black saw his face. He was shocked to see Squash. His heart skipped a beat. The arrhythmia held him in place. Black tried to reach out.

"You left me," said Squash. "Why did you leave me?"

Black could not get any words from his mouth. He shouted but nothing came out.

"It's cold and dark," said Squash. "I am alone, except for the worms, as they feed on my bones."

Black struggled against the invisible force that held him. He fought with all his might but remained mute and motionless. His mind was anchored and his tongue was tied.

"Why brother, why?" pleaded Squash.

An upheaval of earth materialized before Black. The boy's form was enveloped by an all-encompassing soil. It consumed Squash and dragged him below the dirt. Black was powerless. In a forced nuclear reaction, Black released one word. "No!" The thunderclap of his voice echoed throughout the darkness in a blast wave. The thermal pulse flashed over Squash in a fireball. Black watched in horror as his little brother ignited into incendiary screams of terror and pain. The remaining anatomy ionized and burned to ash.

Black awoke in a cold sweat. He caught his breath. The dream was disturbing. He walked around to clear his head. Sober and alert, Black ate to help improve his mental state. He fed Demon and rode onward. It was difficult to concentrate and he found himself completely off course. Haunted by visions at night, and tortured by his actions during the day, Black was stripped bare. He needed to pack away the killing. He needed to find kindness again. Black retreated from the days of death.

The days were still warm but the nights grew cold. Black gazed at the stars and wondered what would become of him. He desired to do good. He could be benevolent and still make a difference. A positive change was needed. The new conviction gave him confidence. He stopped the fighting.

Black followed the railroad until he reached a log cabin village. To its east, was Camp Sumter, a Confederate prison. Sumter was a garrison of wood. It had four walls of fifteen-foot pine that enclosed twenty-six thousand men over twenty-six acres. The pen barely allotted each man the dimensions of a pine box. This detention camp was a death factory.

At the southern tip of the stockade, Black rode up to the officer's house on the hill. He strode into Captain Wirz's post with a perfectly forged copy of papers. Captain Wirz was a small, thin man with a slender nose. His hair was dark, wavy, and receding. A pair of sunken eyes sat above a full beard. He did not smile because there was no reason to do so. Black presented the orders of Commissary General Winder to him. Wirz scarcely glanced at the folded scribblings on the notice.

"First Lieutenant Jonathan Green reporting," said Black.

"You can throw a tent with the boys next door," said Wirz.

Black scowled. He slipped Wirz a one-hundred dollar Union bill. The print on the currency showed a picture of an eagle with wide spread wings. Wirz glared at the greenback.

"It is worth more than Confederate money," said Black.

"Where did you get this?" asked Wirz.

"Off a dead Yank," replied Black.

Wirz placed his hand on the hundred and slid it across the desk. He put it directly into his pocket.

"Go find any log cabin in town, Lieutenant," said Wirz. "Report for duty tomorrow before seven."

Black presented himself the next morning at the north gate. A private saw the two bars on his collar and gave a salute. Black returned the same recognition to the guard.

"Open the gate," said Black. "I am here to review the company."

"Yes, Sir," said the private. "They are about to serve rations right now."

Black moved into a holding area inside the gate. The doors closed behind him like the lid of a coffin. Black got a chill as he looked upon the inside entrance. He imagined a script above the portal. 'Abandon All Hope,' it read. The reinforcement bar was lifted and the barrier was opened to a sideshow of horrors. He saw a line of skeletons in rags waiting for their allotment. Some had almost no clothes. The prisoners stood shoulder to shoulder as far as he could see. Those who were not waiting roamed randomly about. Vermin ran through the camp everywhere. When a man sat, he was instantly covered in lice. Some of the captives lay quietly on the ground. They were so silent that it was difficult to tell if they were alive or dead. The guards gave out less than a half tin cup of dry food. The meal was crushed corn. Much of it was unedible because it contained the cob along with the kernels.

Black looked around at the walls of the stockade. Every ninety feet were raised pigeon roost towers. From there they kept an eye on the men in the cage. Encircling the earth below was the dead line. This small rail marked nineteen feet out from the wall. If any man crossed it, he would be immediately shot and killed. There was no grass. The hard dirt was cloaked with old clothes, men, and shebangs. Most shanties were constructed of two triangular sticks in front and one in the back. A blanket or coat was draped on top, which provided only minimal protection from the elements.

Black strolled down the main street and along the checkerboard thoroughfare. A single stream ran through the center of the camp and into a swamp. The water source was polluted with waste. Spume of oils, char, and fat residue was poured in at its origin by Confederate cooks. Film from bathing and human excrement added to the sludge. The sewage created an increasing number of inmates to become ill. Dysentery, dropsy, and death followed. Scurvy darkened the inmate's mouths. Teeth fell from their rotten gums and boils broke open over their skin. It was wall-to-wall suffering.

Black walked around the area of the swamp. Lean-tos had been constructed there out of necessity. In some cases, it was because there was no more room. In other instances, the prisoners were simply unwanted. Nobody sought to reside beside an infected marsh of mush. These men had been forced from the inclined dirt down into a muddy sunken scum sink. The air was filled with biting mosquitoes. The ground was covered by squirming maggots. The stench was even worse. These poor souls have no recourse. Black looked upon them and saw that even the worst place on earth had a hierarchy. He was saddened by it all.

Black decided to investigate the circumstance. He wanted to help. Many men were near death. Some passed away without notice, unless their clothing was stolen. Black was in charge of the dead. He assigned prison parolees to identify, remove, and bury them. Upon identification, a piece of paper was attached to them with the soldier's name written on it. He was then taken to the Dead House outside the stockade walls. From there, they were transported to the burial trenches north of the compound. The plots were six feet wide and side-by-side. Each grave was marked by a numbered stake. The corresponding number was written on the pinned paper containing their name. At the end of the day, it was delivered to Atwater, a parolee at the Dead House. He logged the names and numbers for the cemetery.

Along the edge of the swamp, Black came upon an appalling scene. Three raiders were beating an older black man right out in the open. No one moved to stop the attack. Enraged by the brutality, Black acted. He tossed the assailants aside like bad fish from a barrel of brine.

"Are you hurt?" Black asked the prisoner.

"'What is thy servant, that thou shouldest look upon such a dead dog as I am?'" he asked. (2Sam 9:8).

"Just asking if you are hurt," said Black.

"No," said the prisoner.

"Go clean yourself up," said Black.

"Thank you, Sir," he said.

"It is Lieutenant," said Black.

"May I ask your name, Lieutenant?" he asked.

"What does it matter?" asked Black.

"Names mean something," he replied.

"Is that so?" questioned Black.

"Yes," he replied.

"Well then, tell me, what is your name?" asked Black.

"Silas," he replied.

"So, you are some kind of missionary?" inquired Black.

"Of sorts," said Silas.

"How so?" asked Black.

"I was born a slave," he started. "As a small child my father smuggled me out of New York and into Pennsylvania. There, I was given to a Quaker family. They raised me free, and as one of their own. I was taught to read and write. The Quakers had only one book, the Bible. When I was older, I preached the Word to the people. When the war broke out, I joined as a minister to the troops. But I was captured and sent here. So you see, I do believe names mean something."

"My name is Jonathan Green," said Black.

"Green," said Silas. "I can see that. I have never seen such brilliant green eyes before."

Black stood like a statue.

"And Jonathan?" continued Silas. "In the Bible, he was a warrior prince. He was the faithful friend of the king. This I can also see in you. See, names mean something."

Black was made uncomfortable by the assessment. He turned away from further inquiries. After a thought, Black reversed himself.

"Silas," said Black. "I have decided to give you a work parole. You will serve at the cemetery burying the dead. I will return tomorrow to collect you. The dig is hard work but at least you should be safe there."

"I know I will be, Lieutenant Green," said Silas.

The next morning, Black went from Andersonville to Camp Sumter. He entered the formidable fortress early that day. He found Silas in the exact same spot as before.

"Time to work," said Black.

Silas stood up. He was dirty and barefoot. He brushed the dust off his clothes and looked at Black.

"Where are your shoes?" asked Black.

"Oh," said Silas. "They double as my pillow at night."

Black marched Silas outside the gate without worry of peril from the pigeon roosts. Once they were far from eyesight, Black gave Silas a canteen of water and a few baked goods.

"What's all this?" asked Silas.

"I will not have you dying on me old man," replied Black.

"That is a real comfort, Sir," said Silas sarcastically.

Black and Silas joined the other paroled prisoners at the gravesite. The bodies had already piled up for burial. Silas saw the attached pieces of paper used for authentication. A stack of small stakes were nearby. It was unnerving.

"You need to dig down four feet into the trench," said Black. "After the body is placed take the name from the clothes and document the number of the stake. At quitting time, take the names and the stake numbers to Atwater at the Dead House.

"Yes, Lieutenant," said Silas.

Silas immediately got to work. He took care to legibly write on each marker. Black pushed him to move faster.

"Why do you take so much time?" asked Black.

"Good penmanship is like one man's actions in a war," said Silas. "Nobody takes notice but it is not insignificant."

"I see," said Black.

"It is the small things that make worth of a man," said Silas.

"Keep working," said Black.

At the end of light, nearly one hundred men had been entombed. Days passed. They were warm days for wintertime. A fierce storm came upon them during the dig. The sky opened and the rain fell like a river. Silas was at the bottom of the pit. He was dragged down by the crumbling walls of mud. The landslide prevented his escape. His attempts to stand sunk his feet even deeper. He slipped below the water and was swallowed by a deadly devouring clay. Black saw all the men leap from the trench except for Silas. He called out for him. There was no answer. Black ran the length of the channel. At one end he saw Silas buried to his torso as the wash rolled over him. Black laid at the edge of the ditch and reached out his left hand. The precipitation had made everything slick. As Silas grabbed Black's gloved hand, the covering came off and Silas slid back. Black dove his arm down into the mixture. He clasped him by the scruff and pulled Silas to safety. Both men lay supine for a time in the pouring rain. Silas gasped to catch his breath. He looked over and saw the mark of the cross on Black's palm. The men got up and moved under the shelter of a large tree.

"Thank God for you," said Silas. "'God is our refuge and strength, a very present help in trouble.'" (Psm 46:1).

"Yes, He is," said Black.

"And you should know that," said Silas.

"Meaning?" asked Black.

"Your hand," said Silas. "You are the Black Death."

Black turned away. "Why would you say that?" he asked.

"I have heard the stories," said Silas. "You are God's avenger. You fight for freedom."

"You are mistaken," said Black. "I am a prison guard."

"Then why are you here, Jonathan Green?" asked Silas.

Black remained silent. He put his left hand into his right and covered the cross. He became dispirited as he stared up into the heavens.

"I am lost," said Black.

"Why?" asked Silas in sympathy.

"My heart," said Black. "I injured my heart."

"I get it," said Silas. "I thought my purpose was to spread the Word of God. When I was captured and brought here, I lost faith. My life seemed meaningless. So I prayed. I prayed every night. I prayed for a miracle. Yet all I received was a wasteland. In August, a giant storm hit here. It was much worse than this one. The clouds were black and the thunder shook the ground. Lightning bolts of immeasurable length shattered the sky. I was terrified. I believed I would die in obscurity and my life would end in nothingness. I watched the clouds cover the camp as my life faded into the immaterial. But morning did come. I was aroused that day by a commotion at the north wall. I ran to see what was happening. When I arrived, I saw a spring of freshwater bubbling from the rock. You, my friend, are like that bubbling stream. You are Providence. I know that you are. And I know why I was sent here now. I was sent here to help you."

"I am not a deliverer," said Black. "I am just a man."

"That is how God does it though," said Silas. "He starts with just one man."

Black noticed that the rain has stopped.

"You need to return to camp," he said to Silas.

"Don't give up," said Silas. "God hasn't given up on you. Let me give you this passage, my friend. 'I therefore, the prisoner of the Lord, beseech you that ye walk worthy of the vocation wherein ye are called.'" (Eph 4:1).

Silas and Black's comings and goings did not go unnoticed. Enlisted soldiers saw Silas receiving special treatment. The guards held hatred in their hearts. They relished watching the parolees work. But any evidence of a reward was abhorrent. This was made clear by the shouts and jeers toward the prisoners as they traveled to their worksites. Black minimized the ire directed at Silas through intimidation. A frown or a stare seem to make them back down.

Outside of the stockade, Black walked with Silas at the end of the day. A group of five guards approached from the opposite direction. In front was a sergeant. Black made sure not to engage them. The sergeant passed by Silas and drove his shoulder into him with force. It knocked him to the ground.

"Watch it Doyle," said Black sternly.

"He bumped into me," said Doyle angrily.

"That is not how I saw it," said Black.

"You calling me a liar, Green?" asked Doyle.

"Try using, Sir," replied Black.

"You calling me a liar, Sir?" asked Doyle.

The men surrounded Black. Silas quickly got up.

"I am unharmed, Sir," said Silas. "Just an accident."

"Be more careful next time," said a forceful Doyle. "We wouldn't want you to get injured now, would we?"

Black watched the men make off, as he and Silas headed straight for the gate.

"Are you alright?" asked Black.

"Nothing bruised," said Silas. "But I know men like him. He is looking for a fight."

"Those days are over for me," said Black. "It is best we just forget it."

"The past has a way of finding a man, Jonathan" said Silas.

"What are you trying to say?" asked Black.

"God gave you a purpose. Yet you acted like Jonah fleeing from Nineveh," said Silas. "Now you find yourself in the belly of a big fish."

"I do have a purpose here," said Black. "And it is to do good."

"Yes," said Silas. "But is it what God wants you to do?"

"I believe to do good is God's will," said Black.

"Jonathan," said Silas. "I have laid my head on hard earth. I have eaten bugs concealed in burnt cornmeal. My muscles have worn away and my skin falls off. I have pain in every joint. Do you know why I endure? 'My strength is made perfect in weakness.' (2Corn 12:9). God made me suffer for a reason. That reason is you."

Black remained quiet.

"I was like you Jonathan," said Silas. "I lost faith while in this place. Now I see that I am here to put you back on your path. This is my purpose. I am to get Jonah to Nineveh. You must re-enter the war."

"You overestimate my efforts," said Black.

"No, Jonathan," said Silas. "You underestimate God."

Black returned home with the conversation still bouncing

around in his brain. Black slept poorly. He thought about doing what was right. Had he denied God? How can doing good go against God's wishes, he wondered. Silas' words nagged at his consciousness. The sentiment plagued him. Black finally dozed off. He awoke late. He rode Demon to the stockade in a hurry. Black entered the gate and went directly to the corner of the camp where Silas stayed. On arrival, Black found Silas was absent. He turned to a neighboring prisoner to inquire about him.

"Where is Silas?" Black asked the prisoner.

"He left a little while ago with the guards," he said.

"With who?" asked Black.

"Sergeant Doyle, I think," he replied.

Black ran from the scene. At the gate he whistled for Demon. Black lept on his back and galloped towards the woods north of the cemetery. Demon went into a sprint. Black pushed him harder in his desperation. He eased up as he came upon a small clearing. He pulled back on Demon's forward power. He saw Silas sitting on a horse with his hands tied. Above him was a rope secured to the branch of a tree. The end was wrapped around his neck. Black jumped from Demon when the men saw him approach.

"Stop this Doyle!" Black screamed.

"Why should you care?" asked Doyle.

"We are guards," said Black. "We have a duty."

"My duty is to the Confederacy!" yelled Doyle.

Doyle struck the rump of the horse. Silas was left to swing. Black grabbed the axe from Demon's side pack. He threw. The hatchet hit with precision. The rope was severed at the branch, releasing Silas. He dropped to the ground in a heap. Doyle looked at Black and smiled.

"Too late," he shouted.

Doyle pulled out his revolver and squeezed the trigger twice.

"Stop!" Black cried.

The shots hit Silas. Bullets flew. Black charged the five guards with a Bowie knife in each hand. He had gone mad. Black moved right and slashed. He struck down two, then turned. Fearful for his life, one guard ran. The other pointed his weapon and fired. Black gave a whistle and Demon bolted forth. He reared on his hind legs and came down. The guard was crushed under heel and hoof. Doyle shot and ran. Black chased him down and with malice he slew him. He hurried over to Silas. He was alive, but barely.

"Hold on my friend," said Black. "I will get you help."

Silas tried to speak. Black saw the blood flow from his chest. His breathing became labored. He sat him up to ease his apnea.

"What is it?" asked Black.

"I leave you now," said Silas. "Go with the glory of God."

"Hold on," said Black. "Hold on."

In his last release, Silas murmured. "Remember me… Remember me."

Black closed Silas' eyes with his hand. He lifted him up and draped him across Demon. Black walked slowly beside the body as he put distance between himself and the site. He directed Demon deep into the woods. The trees towered above him like columns of a great Greek temple. The shade gave comfort from the burning sun. The green hues imparted a spirit of peace. The tranquility took Black far from a maddening war.

He dug a grave and bound two branches together to form a cross. He etched 'Silas' into the stake and placed it into the earth over his head. Black knelt to pray next to it.

"'The righteous perisheth, and no man layeth it to heart. And merciful men are taken away, none considering that the righteous is taken away from the evil to come. He shall enter into peace,'" said Black. (Isaiah 57:1-2).

Afterwards, he looked full around the forest where Silas lay. Black gazed down at the cross containing the inscription.

"Names mean something," he said.

Black went east. He meant to release his wrath on the progenitors of the war. He left destruction in his wake. Black brought the barbarity of war to the people of the South. His outrage powered the ferocity. The intensity increased at each encounter. The path of extirpation went to South Carolina. It was the state where the betrayal began. In Columbia, its capital, convention delegates came to vote for secession at the First Baptist Church. The Ordinance was passed unanimously before a case of smallpox forced them to Charleston where they signed the document. Black was resolved to strike the pit where the southern snakes first released their venom.

It was nighttime in February. A cold current blew. In the hush of the dark, Demon trotted toward Columbia. Black noticed that the bridges had been made impassable. He made a careful approach. Black realized that one or more armies were likely in the area. He moved as a shadow against the moon. Absorbed in anger, Black lost his focus. A familiar sound pricked his ears. It was the click made by the hammer of a gun being pulled back.

"Halt!" a voice ordered.

Black looked for an exit. A ring of torches fired up around him. The shapes of soldiers reflected at his feet. Thirty Union men stood with weapons ready. Black thought about fighting his way out but that could kill many of his brothers in blue. That he could not do. So he stood silent.

"Rebel," continued the voice. "Get on your knees or we will put you there."

"I am not a Rebel," said Black. "Nor will I kneel."

"Do it or die!" shouted the voice.

"Blaze away!" yelled Black in defiance.

"Hold your arms!" came a loud command.

The sea of blue shirts parted and General Sherman stepped forward.

"Hello Matty," he said.

Sherman turned to his troops. "Put your guns down." The men complied. "No one is going to die here," said Sherman. "Did you hear that Matty?"

"Of course, Uncle Billy," said Black.

"Accompany me to my quarters, Matty," said Sherman.

Black followed Sherman through the gathered horde. Sherman took him to his campaign center.

"I was worried for a minute there," said Sherman.

"I was in no danger Uncle Billy," said Black.

"I meant for my men," said Sherman.

He pointed to an undersized chair. "Have a seat," said Sherman.

Black sat.

"Why are you here?" asked Sherman.

"My job is to win the war," said Black. "Just doing my job."

"I have heard about your job, from Savannah all the way here," said Sherman.

"Do not interfere with my methods, my march, or my men."

"Seems like you could use my help seeing General Wheeler's cavalry continue to beat you at every turn," said Black.

"Let me worry about that," said Sherman.

"And what of Charleston?" asked Black. "You did not torch that town. Is it because you still have a soft spot for it from your time at Fort Moultrie?"

"I could order you back to Washington," said Sherman angrily.

"You know that I only answer to Sam or the president," Black retorted.

"Go home Matty," said Sherman. "Go home to your wife and son."

"No!" shouted Black as he stood. "I will not be dismissed! I will not stop! I will tear down their walls and crush the bones beneath my feet!"

"You have lost control," said Sherman. "Matty, listen to yourself." Sherman paced to the opposite side of the tent. "There is no fight for you here," he said. "And I don't want you to put my men at risk. You need to go before you start something."

"'I am come to send fire on the earth. And what will I, if it be already kindled?'" said Black. (Luke 12:49).

"I see there is no reasoning with you," said Sherman. "Do not cross my path again."

"I will make myself scarce as hen's teeth," said Black.

Black exited the tent and blended into the darkness. But he was far from finished. He stormed out in a fire of emotion. On his way, Black perceived the pair of eyes Sherman sent after him. Black made his withdrawal easy for the spies to detect. He slowed. Sherman's scouts were lulled into complacency. Then he vanished. The great sorcerer of concealment backtracked on the men. In secrecy, Black went behind Sherman's tail and entered the city.

Inside the streets of Columbia, it was quiet. Morning was ready to break. Black hid in plain sight. He checked into a hotel right on the main street. He requested a room on an elevated floor. From his window, he had the advantage of the high ground. Black rested his frame in a wooden rocking chair as the hazy purple aurora of day reflected into his room. Black gently pushed against the spindle. His weight rolled the runners over the floor. He glided in a rhythmic fashion until the movement eased him into sleep.

The bright sun of midday brought Black back to life. He went to the window to get a look at the terrain. He noted large bales of cotton stacked up and down the street. He watched the townspeople and Union soldiers rejoice together. The party was already in full swing. There was drinking, dancing, singing, and all forms of merrymaking. Black was infuriated. He was not about to let this city celebrate after the heinous deeds it had done. He became agitated by the actions of the citizens. And he was repulsed by the sight of Sherman's men joining in. Black saw a day of reckoning coming. And it was coming soon.

Night fell. Black came down from his high position and took a blade to the bundles of cotton. The wind sent the loose fibers into the air. Black ignited the cellulose. The white bolls lofted up and set every boulevard ablaze. Black made his escape. Once outside the city, he turned to see it burn. The cleansing nature of the fire accorded satisfaction to him. This chapter was done.

Chapter TWELVE

'For, behold, the day cometh that shall burn as an oven. And all the proud, yea, and all that do wickedly, shall be stubble.' (Malachi 4:1). The burning of Columbia was a statement by Black. It was also a stick in the eye to Sherman. His old commander's indignation towards him pushed Black beyond his limits. His crusade would not stop. 'With the hoofs of his horses, shall he tread down all thy streets. He shall slay thy people by the sword, and thy strong garrisons shall go down to the ground.' (Ezekiel 26:11). But what had once been a holy war was now even more. It was an abomination. The one and only option was annihilation. His anger grew. 'Violence is risen up into a rod of wickedness. None of them shall remain, nor their multitude, nor of any of theirs. Neither shall there be wailing for them.' (Ezekiel 7:11). Black became a rampaging animal. His wrath, however, was not uncontrolled. He levied a calculated carnage, demolishing everything in his path. He crisscrossed the south. He took the fight away from the eastern theater. The maniacal wild dog went farther, and into Texas. No longer were there eyes to follow him. He had no concern for life. All leaves must pale, he thought. What was it to him if he plucked the pedal while it was still green?

Tired and sweaty, Black paused by a clear stream. The sound of rushing water was calming. Black bent down and pulled the glove from his hand. He stuck his mitts into the brook and cupped them like a bowl. He washed the splattered stains from his face. It was cool and cleansing. It gave him a refreshing feeling of renewal. From across the creek came a loud "Bravo!" It was followed by "That was nicely done." Black raised up in a swift motion. He looked over the grassy field in front of him. All he could see was a large shade tree.

"What do you want?" Black shouted sternly.

"Just admiring your handiwork," came the voice. "So, this is the Black Death in action. Impressive."

Black became guarded after hearing his tag used. He took a defensive measure and drew his gun.

"You are one bad man," said the voice.

"You are wrong," Black shouted back. "I am here to do good."

"No man is good," replied the voice.

"Sometimes bad things must be done to curtail evil," said Black.

"What evil do you speak of good sir?" asked the voice.

"No one should be master of another," replied Black.

"So, a benevolent king or a lord should not be master over another?" the voice asked.

Black paused and thought.

"Who are you?" he asked.

"What is in a name?" asked the voice.

"Names mean something," replied Black.

"I am an observer," said the voice.

"Whose side are you on?" asked Black.

"You dress like a Confederate. Yet you act as if you support the Union," said the voice. "Whose side are you on?"

Black decided to change his tactic.

"Come out and we will see if we agree," he said.

"I hardly believe I can trust a killer," said the voice.

"I only fight for what is honorable and right," said Black.

"So killing is not unlawful?" asked the voice.

"This is war!" shouted Black.

"Do not get me wrong," said the voice. "I admire you. I really do. Turning evil into good takes talent."

Black became more frustrated with each remark. Aggravated, he whistled for Demon. The signal blew through the wind. The trumpeting alarm brought Demon running.

"He will not cross the freshwater," said the voice loudly.

Demon suddenly stopped at the bank. Black looked at him in amazement. He mounted the dark horse but Demon remained unmoved. "What is the matter boy?" Black whispered to him. Demon remained fixed like a fly in honey.

"Your righteous world is not what it seems," shouted the voice. "Do you think you can eradicate all evil? How then can you say that you want this war to end?"

"If you know how to finish it, then say so," challenged Black.

"How do you kill a Gorgon?" asked the voice.

"Cut off its head," said Black under his breath.

"Keep up the good work," laughed the voice loudly.

Black leapt down from Demon. He splashed into the current. He ran up the opposite bank and headed for the tree. Black saw a shadow lurking behind the trunk. He rounded the corner only to find nothing. It was a good trick but he had a better one. Black decided to put an end to the war. He would cut off the head of the snake. He returned to Richmond in a search for Jefferson Davis.

It was spring. Galloping along on Demon's back, Black made good time. His arrival found that Richmond resided in complete devastation. Black was shocked to see the city had seen large-scale destruction. Ghost towers of brick stood where buildings had burned. Some structures were completely leveled. Bridges were destroyed. Roads were piles of debris and rubble. The people rummaged through the remains for mere trinkets, and baubles. Black saw the Union boys in blue patrolling the town. He packed away his greys and approached one of the soldiers.

"Excuse me Sir," said Black slyly.

"I'm a private," said the serviceman. "Not an officer."

"Pardon me," said Black. "I know nothing of the ways of the army. I do have a question though."

"Certainly," said the private.

"What happened to all the Rebels?" asked Black.

"Ran away or gone home I suppose," said the private.

"Why?" asked Black.

"Where have you been living?" asked the private.

"I have been gone for a while," said Black.

"Richmond fell in early April. A week after, Lee surrendered to Grant," said the private. "The Rebels set the city on fire on their way out."

"And Jefferson Davis?" asked Black.

"He fled to Georgia but was captured just a few days back," said the private. "The war is over."

"Do you know where General Grant or General Sherman are now?" asked Black.

"Washington," said the soldier.

"Thank you," said Black.

Black rode on to Washington. He wanted to stop by at the President's residence first. He made his way through the city. Many more people were present than ever before. The population had suddenly exploded. Citizens filled the streets and the public houses were stuffed full.

Black entered the rear of Lincolns' large white house unnoticed. He made his way to the south side of the second level. He saw an adjutant at a desk outside the old cabinet room.

"Pardon me," said Black with hat in hand. "I want to see the president."

"President Johnson has not moved in yet," responded the adjutant.

"I was speaking of President Lincoln," said Black.

The adjutant stood as the color drained from his face.

"I thought everyone knew," he said.

"Knew what?" asked Black.

"President Lincoln is dead. He was assassinated last month. He was killed by John Wilkes Booth," said the adjutant.

Black tried to digest what he had just been fed.

"I'm sorry," continued the adjutant.

Black walked away with his head still swirling.

"Can I help you find a place for the night?" asked the adjutant kindly.

"No, thank you," replied Black.

"All the rooms throughout the city are taken due to the Grand Review tomorrow," he said.

"What review?" asked Black.

"The Grand Review of the Union Army. Everyone is in town for it. President Johnson is to preside over the parade. Both of the armies under General Meade and General Sherman will be marching in the celebration," said the adjutant.

"Where is Sherman's army?" asked Black.

"Camped to the west of the Capital," he said.

"Thanks again," said Black. "I will make sure to avoid that bug hill."

Black disappeared into the dust that puffed from his coat.

It was a beautiful May day, the twenty-third. The morning of the Grand Review had arrived. The presidential viewing box was positioned in front of the residence along Pennsylvania Avenue. The big box was a wooden construct. A large triangular font added color to its center. It was covered by a blue drape with white stars. At its apex was a long pole flying the American flag. On either side of it were decorative solo stars. Near ground level, wooden planks ran in front of the seating. They were wrapped in flags from its middle to each end. Behind the banners, were the tiered benches. And at the very front was a line of soldiers standing at attention. They had rifles with bayonet readied at their sides.

General Meade lead the Army of the Potomac down the street. Black stayed in the background. He could see President Johnson sitting in the most prominent position. General Grant was a few seats down on his right. On Grant's lap was a small boy. He bounced up and down with excitement. General Meade saluted the president, then he joined him and the cabinet members in the stands. The march continued in all its glory.

"Soldier," said Black to a guard behind the dignitaries. "This is an urgent message for General Grant."

Black slipped the soldier a folded piece of paper.

"Deliver this immediately," continued Black.

"Who should I say it's from?" asked the soldier.

"Colonel Quaid," replied Black.

The soldier looked around. He saw no harm in fulfilling the request. And to disobey a direct order could put him in peril. He turned and passed through the stands. He came up behind General Grant and whispered in his ear. Grant gazed over his shoulder without expression. The soldier handed him the note. Grant peered at the open sheet. 'Meet me where Lincoln lived,' it read.

General Grant got up and grabbed his son's hand. The nearby brass questioningly watched him leave.

"The boy has to go out for a minute," said Grant in a hushed tone.

General Grant led the boy from the box. He headed for the presidential estate. Grant entered the building and made his way upstairs. The ambient sunlight made the floor bright. The far corners of the passageways remained in the shadows, however. As General Grant passed an alcove he had a strange sensation. He felt a faint presence. The configuration of a man appeared. It was followed by the reflection of Black's green eyes emerging from the haze.

"Matty?" questioned Grant.

"Surprised to see me Sam?" asked Black.

"Knowing you," said Grant. "No, not at all."

Black stepped out into the light.

"Why the secrecy?" asked Grant.

"I have questions only you can answer," replied Black.

"Very well," said Grant.

General Grant walked down the hall still holding his boy's hand. Black followed. Grant sat the boy down outside an empty room.

"Stay here son," said Grant. "I won't be long."

Grant strolled into an old office. As Black passed by the boy they locked eyes.

"Is that Jesse?" asked Black.

"Yes," replied Grant. "Come inside Matty."

"He seems to be a fine lad," said Black as he shut the entry behind him.

"Yes, he is," said Grant. "Now what is this about Matty?"

"I need to know about Lincoln's assassin," said Black. "Has he been brought to justice?"

"It was John Wilkes Booth," said Grant. "He was reportedly killed."

"And Jefferson Davis?" asked Black.

"He is in prison," replied Grant.

"What about Lee?" asked Black.

"He was paroled along with all the other Confederates."

"Paroled?" questioned Black.

"Yes," said Grant. "The terms of surrender were to send them all home on parole."

"Where is the justice in that?" asked Black angrily.

"Matty it is not your decision," said Grant. "President Lincoln made it clear I was to let them up easy."

"This is unacceptable Sam," said Black raising his voice.

"They are our brothers and our sons, Matty," said Grant. "I feel compassion is required here to help reunite this nation."

"A son's love is not what shot me in the back at Pittsburg Landing. Brotherhood did not fire artillery at my head. The Rebels took up arms against the Union, Sam," said Black.

"You have done your duty for God and country," said Grant. "The war is over, Matty."

"There is always another war, Sam," said Black.

"Look, I am your friend," said Grant. "This is all in the past now."

"And what of justice?" asked Black.

"There has been enough suffering on both sides," said Grant. "It is time to heal."

Black turned his back on Grant. He moved over to the window. He peered out as if his soul had been swallowed by the universe.

"Matty, come join Julia and me for dinner tonight," said Grant.

"Very well Sam," said Black. "You have always been a good friend."

"So it's settled," said Grant.

General Grant reached into his pocket and pulled out a wad of bills. He handed the money to Black. "Here," said Grant. "Go buy yourself some dress blues. You have way more than this due in backpay."

"Thank you Sam," said Black. "I will see you tonight."

"Meet us around six at the Willard Hotel," said Grant.

The evening found Black in full dress uniform. The frock coat was dark blue and double breasted. The royal blue jacket had a high v-neck of gold. It matched the Aurelian shoulder knot insignia. Two rows of eight buttons ran down the chest. A red sash was wrapped around his waist. Black strode in like a tower of Union strength. He approached the maître d' hotel. General and Mrs. Grant were already seated. Black was guided to their table. General Grant stood upon Black's arrival.

"Please Sam," said Black. "Be seated."

Black took Mrs. Grant's hand and bowed slightly. He pressed it gently to his lips.

"Matthan Quaid, Madam," he said.

"A pleasure," said Mrs. Grant. "The General has told me much about you."

Black glanced over at Grant in an inquisitive nature.

"Good to see you again Matty," said General Grant.

"My son called you a mountain with feet," said Mrs. Grant. "I see what he meant."

Black smiled and sat.

"General Sherman called you a plague," she continued. "In jest, I am sure."

"Shall we toast?" asked General Grant trying to change the focus. General Grant poured a glass of champagne for everyone. Black removed the glove from his right hand and took hold of the glass. "To the end of the war," said General Grant as he raised his glass.

Black lifted his glass in salute. He took a small sip. Mrs. Grant followed suit.

"Aren't you going to remove your other glove, Colonel Quaid?" asked Mrs. Grant.

"Sorry Madam," said Black. "It is an old injury."

"From the war?" she asked.

"No Madam," replied Black. "It was from my youth."

"I am terribly sorry, Colonel Quaid," she said.

"No offense Madam," said Black. "I am in no pain. And please, call me Matthan."

"The General said you were the best fighting man he had ever commanded. And one of his most important allies," said Mrs. Grant.

"He is very kind," said Black.

"He said in the most difficult battles you always stood firm and pushed forward," said Mrs. Grant. "How did you put it dear?" she asked the General.

"He who continues to attack wins," said General Grant.

"I remember him telling me that God never surrenders," said Mrs. Grant. "He also said you were a big part of it all. And for that I am truly thankful."

"Thank you, Madam," said Black.

"Tell me, Matthan," she said. "How are you feeling now that you are free from fighting?"

"I guess I am unsure how I feel," replied Black.

"Well I for one am happy the war is over," said General Grant. "I have no fondness for war except as a means of peace. And now I can enjoy the company of family and friends."

"Very true," injected Mrs. Grant. "Do you have family Matthan?" she asked.

"Yes Madam," replied Black. "I have a brother in Philadelphia. I also have a wife and son at home in Illinois."

"Splendid," said Mrs. Grant.

"You should visit your brother on your way home Matty," said General Grant. "It would do you good."

"I may not be welcome in Philadelphia," said Black.

"No matter," said Mrs. Grant. "You will soon be reunited with your family."

"I suppose," responded Black. "But I have some unfinished business first."

"Matty that is not for dinner conversation," General Grant chimed in.

"What is that, Sam?" asked Black.

"You know," said General Grant. "It is old news. Besides we are here to celebrate."

"Maybe I cannot forget so easily," said Black.

"The country is united. Men and women are free. It is what President Lincoln wanted. It is why we fought," said General Grant.

"Yes," said Mrs. Grant. "Forget the war."

A stern expression came across Black's face.

"I cannot. I will not," said Black. "Madam, General, please excuse me."

Black got up from the table and he headed for the exit. Mrs. Grant sprung to her feet and followed him. She came from behind and gently touched him on the arm. Black stopped and looked back.

"Please Colonel," said Mrs. Grant. "Forgive me if I have distressed you."

"No Madam," said Black softly. "You have been a delight. And Sam is a valued friend. We simply disagree and my wounds are still fresh."

General Grant came up to the side of Mrs. Grant.

"Dearest could you wait for me at the table?" he asked.

"Be kind, my love," said Mrs. Grant. "I like this one's face."

Mrs. Grant smiled at Black and excused herself. General Grant took a rigid stance with him.

"Matty you are a friend," he said. "But if you break the law, I will come after you."

"Good to see you too General," said Black.

With that, the mountain moved. Black walked out into the busy streets of Washington and disappeared. He traveled to Richmond. Black tracked Lee's movements. He watched and waited as the general of the Army of Northern Virginia came and went from his residence on Franklin Street. He wanted the South to see Lee's punishment made public. Black wanted to make an impact.

It was a sunny Sunday morning in early June. Black followed Lee to Saint Paul's Episcopal Church. It was a tall structure of worship. The entrance had a triangular top. Eight Corinthian columns faced the front. A slender spire rose from the slanted roof. Three stages of the construct converged at the summit. The first was a solid square. The second stage formed an octagon with alternating circles and squares pressed upon its walls. The third and final section consisted of circular columns.

Black entered the church after Lee. He took a seat near the rear where he could see the entire congregation. Lee sat in the front pews. The parishioners were many. The whole assembly was well-dressed and courteous. Assorted whispers arose from the faithful until the Reverend Dr. Minnegerode appeared. He led the people through prayers and devotions. Black participated but the words gave little comfort to his mind. He swam in the waters of revenge. Reverend Minnegerode started his sermon. As he preached, Black slid back into the past. While occupied by his reflection, someone sat discreetly to his right. Black barely glanced at the well dressed gentleman. He hardly noticed his dark pleated pants or the white cuffs that contrasted his suit. Black ignored him. A feeling of pain began growing in Black's thigh. From the corner of his eye, he glimpsed a hand holding his leg tight. Black's vision followed up his arm and caught his face. He radiated light. His countenance glowed like reflected gold.

"Hello Michael," said Black. "Is this what you did to Jacob?"

He increased the pressure on Black's leg. It started to burn. Black shifted his weight. The discomfort continued and then it turned to torment. Black pulled off the glove from his left hand. He clasped the visitor's wrist. Gaseous particles fumed from the point of contact as the temperature rose.

"Release me or I will break it off at the bone," said Black. He relented and Black pulled back his fiery palm.

"The Avenger of Blood. Destroyer of angels and demons alike," he said with indignation. "You are unworthy."

"Why are you here, Michael?" asked Black.

"I carry a message from the Most High," he said.

"And…" questioned Black.

"You are to go no further," he said.

"Leave me alone," said Black.

"The One has spoken it," he said. "Do you not fear Him?"

"'The fear of the Lord is to hate evil. Pride and arrogancy, and the evil way, and the froward mouth do I hate,'" said Black. (Proverbs 8:13).

"Stop or I will strike you down!" he said.

"Or, I will drag you down with me like the rest of the fallen," said Black.

Tempers heightened. The tension was broken by a well-groomed black man. He came and sat on the other side of Black. His abrupt appearance disrupted the adversaries.

"Hello again, Matthan," said the stranger.

Black recognized him. "Gabriel?" he asked.

"Yes," he replied.

Black calmed himself and gave a gentle smile.

"Do you not love God, Matthan?" asked Gabriel. "Will you not follow his commandments?"

The Reverend Minnegerode prepared to administer the holy

sacraments of bread and wine. Gabriel immediately walked forward to the front of the church. He advanced to the altar and he knelt down to take communion. The congregation was silent. After a very long minute, Robert E. Lee approached the chancel. He knelt next to Gabriel. Without further delay, the remaining churchgoers joined in the sharing. Black watched in amazement. It was like seeing the birth of a brand-new star. He reflected on the mercy of God. Black became filled with gratitude. He was thankful for his blessings. And he was thankful for forgiveness. Black stared as the wonderment of love continued to unfold in front of him. He placed his hat on his head. On his way out, he tipped it to Michael. Then, he went on his way.

Matthan went west. He headed for home. He could almost smell Beatrice's cooking as he rode through the valleys. He thought about seeing his wife again for the first time. Matthan imagined looking across a crowded swanky ball. He saw a swirling ensemble of dancers. On the opposite side of the room was Beatrice. She was smartly dressed in purple. The front of her frock fell from her neck in a crescent moon. The shape was mirrored on the back of the gown. The fashionable sleeves puffed out, then became pinned down near her elbow. Her waist was accentuated by a snug belt. It showed off her figure. The dress ended in a bell of lavender lace all the way to her ankles. Beatrice's elegant white gloves covered her skin up to her forearm. She wore a chandelier necklace of clear stones with matching earrings. Her hair was held high in a taut bun at the top of her head. The bangs and sides were full of waves and curls. Everything seemed to move in a picturesque rhythm.

Matthan saw himself in a coat and tails. The suit was black with a white high-collared shirt. A snow-colored ascot clung to his chest. It was layered and it bulged from his throat like an iceberg. His hair was trimmed and neat. The side was parted and straightened back. At the pinnacle of the styling was a raked cockscomb. Matthan's left hand was gloved. His right was bare, tanned, and calloused.

Matthan weaved through the dancers. He presented his gloved

hand to Beatrice. She put hers into his and with a single step the two floated onto the floor. The chic pair glided across the air in an ethereal kinesis. It was grace on grace. It was poised polish melded to sophisticated strength. They spun as one in debonair confidence. The swing and the sway enhanced their emotions. Their eyes shimmered and their smiles widened and beamed, as they twirled in a ballet of true love.

Matthan's masquerade faded. He walked Demon the remaining few miles and into the barn. Angel stood in the stall next to him. Matthan didn't know who was happier. Both horses seemed excited to see their old friend. Matthan entered the main house. Jacob heard his father and ran from the kitchen.

"Pappy!" he yelled. Matthan squeezed him tight. Beatrice rounded the corner with a joyful smile.

"Get in here," said Matthan.

Beatrice made it an embrace of three.

"You look the same," she said.

"Nothing changes me," said Matthan.

"Come and have something to eat," said Beatrice. "You must be hungry and thirsty from your journey."

"I am my love," said Matthan. "It is good to see you. It is good to be home."

Matthan worked hard on the land. He plowed, planted, watered, and nurtured. A young Jacob followed his father's every footstep. He watched, engaged, and performed. Matthan instructed his boy on farming, hunting, and trapping. Beatrice had loftier dreams for her son. For what she desired, Jacob required a higher education. Therefore, they sent him to Philadelphia for a few weeks to stay with his uncle. He got the instruction and exposure he needed. It also gave Matthan and Beatrice some time alone.

A letter from Washington came in the post. Matthan recognized Sam's handwriting. Inside, it said that General Grant and Julia were to pass by on their way to Galena. There was a dedication for him scheduled soon. General Grant stated that a stop at the ranch would be a much welcomed visit with an old friend. Matthan was happy to get the news. He showed the letter to Beatrice. The stay was eagerly awaited with Jacob away. The Grant's arrival was greeted with great joy. The men shared their war stories. The women spoke of everything else. Matthan felt good seeing his friend.

Months later, Matthan received a second note from Sam. The language inside was a cause for concern.

> Matty,
>
> It is with great regret that I take pen to paper today. Duty and friendship often require one to inform individuals of unwanted occurrences. Believe me, it is not easy.
>
> With my condolences, I must notify you that Red and White have been killed. I am truly sorry to say it my friend. Intelligence tells me that a death warrant has been issued for you and Blue as well. Despite contrary reports, it is a group led by John Wilkes Booth. Do what is best for your family's safety. And for you. Of course, you always have a home in my organization.
>
> Sam

Matthan sadly returned from town. An old ogre from his past had reappeared. His last experience cost him more than anyone knew. Matthan was not fearful of a fight, but now it had gone beyond the battlefield. His household was in jeopardy. For their protection, he decided to remove the threat by faking his death.

At dinner, Matthan was extra quiet. Long strings of silence presided over the meal. Matthan heard the words but wasn't really listening. If he stayed, he could lose them. If he ran, he would lose them. This was not a baby he could split in two.

Beatrice noticed Matthan's detachment. She sent Jacob to bed with a kiss. Then, she sat calmly down.

"What is it dear?" she asked. "I have not seen you like this since the war."

A dread filled Matthan's face. He smiled through the misgiving.

"God gave us free will," he said. "But I find myself with a singular choice."

"That can be difficult to reconcile," said Beatrice. "Pain can cloud a loving path."

"Just choose love," said Matthan. "I wish it was that simple."

"Maybe it is," said Beatrice with a smile of acceptance.

She got up and placed her arms around her husband.

"That is what I did," she said.

"Thank you, my Beloved," said Matthan. "Let me go check on the boy."

Matthan went and sat at Jacob's side. The young boy's nervous energy was still flowing.

"Time to extinguish the light," said Matthan.

"I cannot sleep," said Jacob.

"Why?" asked Matthan.

"I worry," replied Jacob.

"Fall back on your faith son," said Matthan. "God speaks His love to your heart. Listen. God hears you call his name. Pray."

"I will Pappy," said Jacob.

"Do that and you will grow to be a good man," said Matthan.

"Pappy," said Jacob. "You were in the war."

"Yes," said Matthan.

"Uncle said war is bad," said Jacob.

"Yes," replied Matthan.

"And he said killing is bad," said Jacob.

"Yes, it is," said Matthan.

"Are you a good man or a bad man?" asked Jacob.

"Yes," replied Matthan.

Matthan put out the flame with his fingers. All became dark.

"Go to sleep son," he said.

Matthan lay motionless until Beatrice fell asleep. He dressed and went to the barn. He saddled Demon and said goodbye to Angel. Matthan led Demon out the back. He returned and set alight the hay. The fiery reflections flickered and danced on the ground. Matthan heard the door to the house slam closed. He ran outside to inquire.

"Pappy! Pappy!" shouted Jacob.

Matthan met him halfway and reached out his arms. He placed them on Jacob's shoulders and bent down to one knee.

"Jacob," he said. "I need to go in there and free the horses. Otherwise, they will die. Do not worry son, I will be fine."

"Let me help," said Jacob.

"No," said Matthan. "Fire is a dangerous foe. It is unpredictable in its advance. I must go in alone."

Matthan looked at the barn, then at his son.

"I want you to round up Angel and Demon after I set them free. They will be afraid and likely run. I want you to corral them. Can you do that for me son?" he asked.

"Yes," said Jacob.

"Isaiah said it best. 'Fear thou not for I am with thee. Be not dismayed, for I am thy God. I will strengthen thee, yea, I will help thee, yea I will uphold thee with the right hand of my righteousness,'" said Matthan. (Isaiah 41:10).

Matthan went back to the door. Small spot fires sprang up all around the outside. Matthan ran into the burning barn. He felt the extreme heat on his skin. The thermal convection forced him to squint. He released Angel from her stall. She fled, running at full steam.

The height of the flames reached the roof and crowned. The rollover ignited the gases. Sparks and crackles sounded from the supports. The climbing conflagration obliterated the walls around him. The ceiling exploded and fell. The singed materials came down upon Matthan's head. The blow knocked him to his knees.

He was stunned. He saw the scene in front of him start to distort. All the lines curved. Colors combined like a kaleidoscope. Matthan struggled to maintain consciousness. He felt the strange sensation of falling. It was as if a large hole had opened below him. Looking down, he saw only darkness. Before him was his old battle axe, just out of reach. He strained to get his hand on the weapon. The more he tried the farther away he would slide. In desperation, he blurted out a breathless murmur.

"'O my God, take me not away in the midst of my days,'" he said. (Psm 102:24).

Matthan closed his eyes to clear the smoke. He opened them and saw a single ruby-throated hummingbird. The wings fluttered at great speed. His avian companion hovered with his head slightly cocked in curiosity.

"Come to me, have you?" asked Matthan.

He felt his soul slip from reality. Matthan reached for the bird. His downward momentum stopped. His path reversed. Matthan was pulled from the pit. His blurry field came into focus. At once, Matthan saw his left hand holding the handle of the axe. He exerted himself to the maximum. Getting up, he yanked the axe from its anchor. He crashed out the back with a swing. He wrangled Demon and rode away, undetected.

The integrity of the barn was lost and the remnants burst and crumbled. The coals glowed for hours afterward. The mounds of grey dust cooled over time leaving the likes of a Rorschach test on its surface. At morning's light, Jacob again returned to the site. He sat and stared at the pattern. Disordered thoughts left him confused as to the interpretation of the night's events. One life ended and one life had begun.